DOWN ON GILA RIVER

Center Point
Large Print

Also by Ralph Compton and Joseph A. West
and available from Center Point Large Print:

The Burning Range
The Last Manhunt
The Stranger from Abilene
The Ghost of Apache Creek

**This Large Print Book carries the
Seal of Approval of N.A.V.H.**

Ralph Compton

DOWN ON GILA RIVER

A Ralph Compton Novel
by Joseph A. West

CENTER POINT LARGE PRINT
THORNDIKE, MAINE

This Center Point Large Print edition
is published in the year 2013 by arrangement with
NAL Signet, a member of Penguin Group (USA) Inc.

This is a work of fiction. Names, characters,
places, and incidents either are the product of
the author's imagination or are used fictitiously,
and any resemblance to actual persons,
living or dead, business establishments, events,
or locales is entirely coincidental.

The text of this Large Print edition is unabridged.
In other aspects, this book may vary
from the original edition.
Printed in the United States of America
on permanent paper.
Set in 16-point Times New Roman type.

ISBN: 978-1-61173-765-3

Library of Congress Cataloging-in-Publication Data

West, Joseph A.
Down on Gila River : a Ralph Compton novel / Joseph A. West and
Ralph Compton.
pages ; cm.
ISBN 978-1-61173-765-3 (library binding : alk. paper)
1. Large type books. I. Compton, Ralph. II. Title.
PS3573.E8224D69 2013
813´.54—dc23

2013003355

THE IMMORTAL COWBOY

This is respectfully dedicated to the "American Cowboy." His was the saga sparked by the turmoil that followed the Civil War, and the passing of more than a century has by no means diminished the flame.

True, the old days and the old ways are but treasured memories, and the old trails have grown dim with the ravages of time, but the spirit of the cowboy lives on.

In my travels—to Texas, Oklahoma, Kansas, Nebraska, Colorado, Wyoming, New Mexico, and Arizona—I always find something that reminds me of the Old West. While I am walking these plains and mountains for the first time, there is this feeling that a part of me is eternal, that I have known these old trails before. I believe it is the undying spirit of the frontier calling me, through the mind's eye, to step back into time. What is the appeal of the Old West of the American frontier?

It has been epitomized by some as the dark and bloody period in American history. Its heroes—Crockett, Bowie, Hickok, Earp—have been reviled and criticized. Yet the Old West lives on, larger than life.

It has become a symbol of freedom, when there was always another mountain to climb and another river to cross; when a dispute between two men was settled not with expensive lawyers, but with fists, knives, or guns. Barbaric? Maybe. But some things never change. When the cowboy rode into the pages of American history, he left behind a legacy that lives within the hearts of us all.

—Ralph Compton

DOWN ON GILA RIVER

Chapter 1

A fifty-year-old, stove-up puncher with the rheumatisms and shortsighted eyes has no right to pick a fight with a bunch of young bronco Apaches.

Sam Sawyer was aware of that rule, but since the Indians had done the pickin' he figured he was in the right.

Not that it mattered.

The Mescaleros already had his pony, saddle, and rifle, and now they were after his scalp. All things considered, Sam figured he was in a difficult situation. He still had his Colt but couldn't hit anything with it unless at spitting distance, and the Apaches weren't about to get that close.

Already their rifle bullets hit nearer. Accompanied by a spiteful whine, they chipped rock from the top of the boulder that concealed him or rattled through the juniper on the higher ground just above his head.

He was, Sam decided, truly between a rock and a hard place.

But desperate times require desperate measures. By nature Sam Sawyer was a talking man and he figured he might be able to silver-tongue his way out of this fix.

Where bullets had failed, words could succeed.

9

"Hey, you Injuns down there," Sam yelled. "Jes' leave my pony an' saddle and we'll forget this shootin' scrape ever happened. How does that set with you, huh?"

The only reply was a flurry of shots that forced Sam to hit the ground, his heart thudding like a trip-hammer in his chest.

He learned a great truth that day: when Apaches wanted to lift a man's scalp, they weren't much on polite conversation.

Slowly, Sam lifted his head and peered over the boulder. He saw the three Indians moving around farther down the talus slope, just a fleeting moment of a glimpse, and then they were gone again.

Sam thumbed off a shot, taking a pot to keep the Indians honest. He saw a pad leap off a prickly pear cactus, but then his bullet chattered harmlessly into the underbrush.

Answering shots whined off the rock, and one of them drove splinters into Sam's left cheek, drawing blood and a startled curse. He dived for the ground again, still cussing.

An optimistic man, Sam spat out dirt and dried leaves and tried to look on the bright side. But try as he might, there was no bright side—nary a happy ending in sight.

"Dang," he said, talking aloud, the habit of men who ride lonely trails, "I reckon you're done fer this time, Sam'l."

• • •

Sam Sawyer was holed up in the rugged breaks at the foot of New Mexico's Haystack Mountain in the high desert country. Spreading away from him lay a brush valley that pointed like an arrowhead toward what had been his destination, the Silver City boomtown.

He'd figured that he might prosper there, perhaps in the restaurant business, since a ranch cook had once told him, "Sam, I reckon you can fry an egg and burn a steak with the best of them."

But hard fate had intervened and his prospects were blighted.

Sam had been riding south from the Spur Lake Basin country when the Apaches jumped him, scared his horse, and left him afoot.

Now pinned to the break like a butterfly to a board, he could only wait and wonder when the Indians would make their move.

There was an almost impassible thicket of brush and cactus to his left, and to his right another pile of rock that had tumbled down the mountain during some ancient earth-shake. Behind him rose a sheer slope, so he was confident that no attack would come from that direction.

Sam took time to build a cigarette and shook his head. The Apaches were taking their own sweet time, content to make a man die a hundred deaths before the real thing happened. The day was blistering, the sun a white-hot coin in the cloudless sky. Ravens quarreled in the junipers, raining a shower of twigs, cones, and needles. Close to Sam, a swallowtail butterfly circled close to a purple bull thistle, then fluttered away in tattered flight.

A probing arrow thudded into the slope behind Sam, then a second.

Angry now, he cupped a hand to his mouth and shouted, "Hey, you buzzards! You're gonna put somebody's eye out!"

There was no answering shout, nor further arrows.

Sam peered over the rim of the boulder again. Nothing moved and there was no sound.

Maybe the Apaches were gone. The arrows might have been a last act of defiance, calculated to make the white man wet his pants.

If that was the case, they'd almost succeeded.

A minute dragged past slowly, heavy with heat.

Still nothing moved and only insects made their small sounds in the grass.

Emboldened, Sam stood. And drew an instant fusillade.

A bullet jerked off his hat and another tugged at his left sleeve. He dived for the ground again and yelped as one of his rheumatic knees slammed against a buried rock.

Dang, that was going to hurt later. If there was a later.

His knee paining him, Sam's anger again flared. He jumped up and fanned his Colt dry. Then he holed up behind the boulder again.

A derisive laugh rose from the flat in front of him, his wild shots tickling some Apache's sense of humor.

Sam took shells from his cartridge belt and fumbled six into the chambers of his revolver.

His canteen hung from his saddle horn, wherever that was now, and thirst had begun its slow torment. His mouth was as dry as mummy dust, and his red-rimmed eyes felt gritty in the sun glare.

He rubbed his aching knee, angry that the Apaches were not giving up, angry with himself for leaving the security of the Rafter-T, and hazarding what was left of his future on a wild adventure to Silver City.

He was too old for wild adventures, and the Mescaleros were busy making that obvious.

But fate can be as flighty as a sixteen-year-old girl at her first cotillion.

And now it intervened on Sam Sawyer's behalf.

Bronco Apache warriors, especially Chiricahua, were the most notional people on this green earth. And they proved that now.

When Sam looked over the boulder rim, all three Apaches had mounted their ponies in full view of him—a comment on what they thought of his marksmanship—and one of them, wearing the yellow headband of a former army scout, led his saddled mustang.

Sam didn't need to think about it—the fact was obvious that they were giving up the fight and moving on.

He was mightily puzzled over the why of the thing.

But, rack his brain as he might, he came up with no answer. Though he thought up a few maybes.

Maybe they figured the mustang, saddle, and rifle were booty enough and it was not worth getting killed or wounded just to murder a gray-haired white man. Maybe they were homesick for their *rancheria* and their wives and young'uns. Maybe they'd gotten a sudden attack of the croup.

Maybe a lot of things.

But they were leaving and that was enough to bring a smile to Sam Sawyer's craggy, weather-beaten face.

So puffed up was he in this reversal to his fortune that he stepped clear of the boulder and yelled, "Hey, you! Leave that dang mustang hoss right where it's at."

The Apache in the yellow headband drew rein and stared at Sam for a long time, his black eyes glittering. Then he bent over on his pony's back and slapped his rear with the flats of his hands.

Now Sam knew he'd been insulted, both as a man and a warrior, but he did nothing. He wasn't a good enough shot to hit the Mescalero's backside, and a miss would only make the Apaches mad and stir things up again.

So he just stood and watched the Apaches leave. He could still hear them laughing at him long after he could no longer see them.

Thus it was that Sam Sawyer, in low spirits, came down from the breaks and onto the flat. He had no horse, no water, and no food—and it was a long, long way to Silver City.

Sam walked for an hour and amused himself by kicking a rock, keeping it in front of him, retrieving it from under cactus or brush, then toeing it forward again. His shadow grew longer and his feet had started to ache when he stumbled on a narrow stream that branched off from Sacaton Creek.

The water was warm and brackish, but Sam drank deep, then fetched his back against a cottonwood, built a cigarette, and considered his situation. In truth, he had little to consider. By his recollection, Silver City lay about forty miles to the south, tucked into a rocky cradle of rugged mountains, ravines, and mesas. Even for a walking man it was a fur piece, and, like every cowboy ever born, Sam Sawyer was not a walking man.

His store-bought boots had cost him four dollars and seventy-five cents three years before and were much scuffed and down-at-heel, and easy enough on the feet. But they'd been made tight and narrow on a horseman's last, and hiking in them had never entered the boot maker's thinking.

Now, as Sam's feet swelled, the boots pinched, scraped, and crushed his toes into tangled knots and he couldn't pull them off because he feared he wouldn't get them back on again.

Thus, as he smoked his cigarette and pondered his plight, Sam Sawyer was not in the best frame of mind. He carried a horse chestnut in one pocket to ward off the rheumatisms and in the other a dried rattlesnake heart for consumption. But they brought him little comfort.

He again cussed himself for leaving the Rafter-T. Like many a puncher before him with arthritic knees and a spine jarred too often by half-broke ponies, he'd been offered, and accepted, the job of assistant cook.

Looking back—dang, was it just three weeks ago?—Sam decided that a man should never turn his back on a job that offered plenty of grub, a comfortable bunk, and free whiskey every Friday night, plus a handsome salary of thirty a month.

He glanced at the sky where the sun was beginning its drift to the west and he took on a philosophical turn of mind. What was it his ma always said? Oh yeah, she'd say, *"Samuel, it's no use crying over spilt milk."* Well, Ma was right. He'd chosen his way and now he'd have to stick to it without regret.

He'd made up his mind, but Sam figured that up until now Ma's advice sure hadn't helped much.

Chapter 2

Hannah Stewart walked back to her cabin, a basket of brown eggs hanging from one arm, but stopped a few feet short of the door as a distant movement across the brush flats caught her attention.

The flats shimmered in the late summer sun, and dust drew a fine veil over the distance. She laid the basket at her feet and shaded her eyes against the glare. Her gaze reached far and finally rested on the moving speck that grew in size as it slowly came nearer.

Beyond the flat rose the purple peaks of the Mogollon Mountains that stretched westward to the Arizona border, a ragged rampart against the blue haze of the sky.

Hannah glanced away, rested her eyes, and once again returned her gaze to the approaching . . . figure.

Yes, it was a man, no doubt about that. An Apache?

The woman dismissed the thought. The man didn't move like an Indian. Rather, he had a hesitant, high-stepping gait, like somebody walking barefoot on nettles.

Hannah felt a tug on her skirt.

"Is it Pa?" her daughter asked, her brown eyes wide and as round as copper coins.

A pang of something akin to sadness stabbed at Hannah Stewart's heart. "No, Lori," she said, "it's not Pa." She took the child's hand. "We're going inside," she said.

"Let me carry the eggs," Lori said.

"I think they're too heavy for you, honey."

"No, they're not. I'm a big girl now. I'm four."

"Three."

"Nearly four."

Hannah smiled. "All right, carry the basket, but be careful."

She opened the door wide for the child, and then glanced back at the man on the trail.

A white man. Big hat, knee-high boots, a gun on his hip.

A cowboy, then. Or an outlaw.

Hannah helped Lori put the eggs on the table. Then she took the shotgun from above the fireplace. She crossed the floor to a cupboard, opened the drawer, and took two bright red shells from a box.

She loaded the Greener and turned to Lori. "Shh," she said, forefinger to her lips. "Be a little mouse until I come back."

The girl looked at her mother in alarm and Hannah smiled.

"It's only a cowboy searching for his lost horse," she said. "I'll go talk to him, is all."

"Be careful, Mommy," Lori said, her voice trembling a little.

"I will," Hannah said. "Now, remember, be a quiet little mouse."

She stepped outside—just as Sam Sawyer reached the well. Hannah saw the man's eyes move over her, from her face to her breasts to the swell of her hips under her plain gray work dress.

She found nothing offensive in the man's gaze. He'd looked at her without heat, as a man will look at any attractive woman.

Sam touched the brim of his battered black hat. "Howdy, ma'am," he said. "I wonder if I can trouble you for a drink of water."

Hannah nodded. "Yes, please help yourself."

She watched as the man dropped the bucket into the well, heard the splash and then saw him raise it again.

"There's a dipper on a nail beside you," she said.

"Obliged, ma'am," Sam said.

He drank deep, drank again, and when Hannah

figured the worst of his thirst had been quenched, she said, "Have you come far?"

"Yes, ma'am, from the mountains back there. Apaches made off with my hoss and nearly my hair."

He drank again, then said, "Afore that, I was working fer the Rafter-T, up in the Spur Lake Basin country."

Anticipating the woman's next question, he said, "Name's Sam Sawyer, an' I'm headed fer Silver City." He smiled, showing his teeth. "I figured I might prosper there in the restaurant profession."

"My name is Hannah Stewart," the woman said. "This is my place."

She was not yet sure she could trust this man and didn't mention Lori. But she had dropped the shotgun barrels so the muzzles pointed at the ground.

Sam's eyes swept over the cabin, the out-buildings, and then lingered on the barn. "Live here by yourself, ma'am?" Sam asked.

Hannah hesitated a moment. "Yes. My husband rode away three months ago and I haven't seen him since. I expect he'll be back at any time now."

She saw Sam nod, but he didn't comment.

As he had studied her, now the woman sized up her visitor.

He was a stocky man, about average height. His face was deeply lined and weathered, his eyebrows untrimmed and craggy, as was his great dragoon mustache. His teeth when he smiled were white, unusual for the high desert country where dentists were few and far between, and his blue eyes were bright and good-humored, as though he found everything in the world around him amusing.

He wore scuffed, work-worn jeans and wide canvas suspenders over a faded blue shirt. His cartridge belt and the holster that carried a walnut-handled Colt were much worn but of obvious good quality.

Hannah put the man's age at sixty, but figured he could be older, or younger. She decided to take a chance on the man named Sam Sawyer.

"Are you hungry?" she said. "I was about to cook supper for my daughter and me."

"Little blond gal with big brown eyes, huh?" Sam said.

"Yes. But how did you—"

"She's been lookin' at me out the window since I got here, ma'am," Sam said, grinning.

Hannah thought the man had a good smile, friendly and open, as though he had nothing to hide.

"Her name is Lori," she said. "She worries about her ma."

"And why shouldn't she, ma'am?" Sam said. "I mean, a right handsome woman like you all alone in this wilderness."

Immediately Hannah became defensive again.

"Not so alone, Mr. Sawyer," she said. "The local cowboys stop by often, especially if they smell doughnuts in the wind. And Sheriff Moseley visits when he's in the area."

"Sheriff?" Sam said. "You mean he rides all the way up here from Silver City?"

The woman shook her head. "No. South of here there's a small cow town on Mogollon Creek called Lost Mine, and Vic Moseley is its sheriff."

Sam peered to the south. "Dang, I don't see it."

"If you walk up the rise there, you'll see it," Hannah said. "It's only a couple of miles away." She hesitated, and then said, "It isn't much of a town."

Sam nodded. "Is the invitation to supper still open, ma'am?" he said. "I'm feelin' famished, an' no mistake."

Hannah smiled. "Of course it is."

Chapter 3

"He was a great warrior," the old Apache said. "The bravest of the brave, skilled in war. He had many horses."

"And now he is dead, Grandfather," the boy said.

"Yes, Goso is dead. Killed by the Mexicans in a great battle."

"Then why do we seek him?"

The old Apache was silent for a while, his deeply wrinkled face still, though he sat his pony and pondered the boy's question. Finally he said, "His soul has lost its way and does not know how to reach the shadow lands. We will help him, you and I."

"But how, Grandfather?" The boy was ten years old that year and had many questions. He rode a spotted pony as old as he was.

"I will pray to the Great Spirit and ask him to show us the way."

"But why here, in this place?" the boy said. "Or any other place?"

"I had a dream and in my dream I saw this place, the mountains and the plain and amidst it all stood a great tree. Goso sat his pony under the tree and I said to him, 'You must move on to the land of shadows.' I said to him, 'Follow the trail of all the dead buffalo, for it is wide and well marked.' But Goso did not look at me or speak to me and a hawk flew over the tree and made a loud cry and I became very afraid. When I woke, one of my women said, 'You cry out in your sleep, husband.' "

The old warrior was silent for a while. Then he said, "It was the spirit hawk that told me where I would find Goso, and that is why we seek him in this lonely place."

"But, Grandfather, why—"

"Faugh, Nolgee, you wear me out with your questions," the old man said. "Let us ride from the shadow of the mountains and onto the plain, where we will look for the great tree I saw in my dream."

The old Apache and his grandson rode out of the Mule Mountains and headed east under a high sun. The day was hot and the sky was blue as far as the eye could see. Insects made their small sounds in the grass, and the air smelled of pine and mountain wildflowers.

The boy saw the Chiricahua first, three warriors leading a white man's horse. When they drew closer, the one who wore the yellow headband of an army scout drew rein and put field glasses to his eyes. Unlike the other two, that man was painted for war.

Nolgee was much afraid and said, "Grandfather . . ."

"I see them," the old man said. "They are Chiricahua and brothers to the Mescalero."

"Then why do they look at us through the white man's seeing glass?"

"Perhaps they fear us, grandson," the old man said. But he smiled as he said it.

"If they fear us, they will run away," the boy said.

"Then we will wait here and let them come," the old man said. "Or run away as the notion takes them."

But the three warriors came on and when they were yet at a distance they halted their ponies and stared at the old warrior and the boy, and their gaze lingered on the horses they rode.

It occurred to the old Apache then that he and his grandson had good spotted ponies, and he himself carried a fine Spencer carbine, had a Colt holstered at his waist, and wore a necklace of silver Mexican pesos. Such great treasures were worth fighting for.

The warrior with the yellow headband took time to look at all those things, then said, "Where do you go, Grandfather?" And to make his companions laugh, which they did, he said, "Do you take the war trail?"

"I seek a troubled spirit," the old man said. He did not look directly at the warrior because that is not the Apache way. "My grandson rides with me to learn the way of such things."

The warrior's eyes flicked to Nolgee, dismissed him, then said to the old man again, "What is this spirit you speak of?"

"The spirit of a great man of our people, the warrior named Goso. He must be shown the trail to the shadow lands."

"Faugh," the man with the yellow headband said, "Goso was killed by Mexican lancers in a great battle in the foothills of the Sierra Madres. His spirit does not roam the land of the Chiricahua."

The old man sat straighter on his pony and he said, "My name is Tsisnah, and I say it does. Goso sits his pony under a broad tree because he is lost and knows not whether he lives or is dead. I know these things because I saw them in a terrible dream."

The young warrior's face changed, showed surprise. "You are Tsisnah, the brave Mescalero war chief grown old?"

"Not old enough to run from a fight."

Now the two warriors behind the one with the yellow headband whispered one to the other and told of the fierce battles Tsisnah had won and of the many scalps he had taken.

They were very much in fear of him because it was said he could command the lightning and halt the course of the sun so that the day for the battle grew longer.

Speech fled from the man with the yellow headband's mouth, but Tsisnah said, "Will you let us pass? We mean no harm to the Chiricahua or to anyone else. We are travelers."

The young warrior bowed his head, then looked up again and said, "I am a poor man, but I do not envy the things Tsisnah possesses."

"Then you do me great honor."

The warrior reached into the pocket of the white man's black vest he wore and took out a brass compass, the kind the horse soldiers used to find their way because they are poor scouts.

But it was a gift worthy of Tsisnah. He extended the compass to the old man.

"This will help you in your search for Goso," he said. "Night or day, the needle always points to that place in the sky where the North Star dwells. It is a great wonder."

The old man took the compass, stared at it long, then smiled and said, "And again you do me honor." He reached down, unbuckled his cartridge belt, and passed it and the holstered Colt to the warrior.

"This is a small thing, not to be compared with the fine gift you gave me, but take it and remember Tsisnah," he said. "At night when you sit by the fire, tell the people, 'Once I met Tsisnah when he was grown old and he gave me this revolver.' "

The young warrior was very affected by this talk and he showed the blue Colt to his companions and their eyes grew large because Tsisnah had so freely parted with such a valuable weapon.

"May you find the soul of Goso and help him find his way to the shadow lands," the warrior with the yellow headband said. "I will think of you often and pray to Great Spirit for your success."

Then, since the Apache have no word for good-bye, he and his companions rode away until they faded into the shimmering heat and were lost in the distance.

Chapter 4

"That was a right elegant meal, ma'am," Sam Sawyer said, laying his fork on the plate.

"I rather fancy that fried salt pork and beans is far from elegant," the woman said. "But thank you for a most singular compliment."

"Ma," Lori said, openly speaking her thoughts as children do, "why does the man smell so bad?"

Sam saw Hannah flush and he smiled. "I guess I do, little girl," he said. "Three weeks on the trail will do that to a man."

"Why doesn't he take a bath?" Lori said, as loud as before.

She looked at her mother, careful to avoid Sam's amused eyes.

Hannah was flustered, at a loss for words, but Sam supplied them.

"I reckon I'll take a bath and a shave real soon," he said. "How does that set with you, Lori?"

The girl buried her face in her mother's side and said nothing.

"I'm sorry," Hannah said. "Children do speak out of turn."

"No need to apologize," Sam said. "I've been smelling my own sweat for the past week."

He took the makings from his shirt pocket and held them where the woman could see them. "May I beg your indulgence, ma'am?"

"Of course," Hannah said. "My husband was a smoking man, though he favored a pipe."

As he built his cigarette, Sam said, "I learned this from Mexican vaqueros down Texas way. They're much addicted to the habit, as I am." He smiled. "Now I don't know whether to thank them or shoot them on sight."

"I heard a doctor say that tobacco smoke is good for the lungs," Hannah said.

"Heard that my own self," Sam said. "I guess them doctors know what they're talking about."

He studied Hannah through a haze of blue smoke. Miz Stewart was a fine-looking woman, in her late-thirties, Sam reckoned, and the sun had not yet browned and wrinkled her. She was tall, slim-boned with corn-silk hair, and large, expressive brown eyes. She seemed more suited to be a drawing room ornament in an eastern city than a pioneer woman in the high desert country of the New Mexico Territory.

Yet, despite her seeming delicacy, Sam sensed there was iron in Hannah Stewart, tempered to flexible steel by a harsh land and the daily struggle to survive.

Following up on his drawing room notion, he said, "Are you planning to stay on here, ma'am, now your man is gone?"

Hannah hesitated. "I don't know that Tom is gone forever. Maybe he . . . maybe . . ." Her voice trailed off into a near whisper. "Well, maybe a lot of things."

Sam said nothing, watching the woman, the sudden lost look in her eyes.

After a few moments, Hannah said, "To answer your question, we, Lori and me, will be out of here before winter."

"You have a place to go?"

"No."

"Money? You'll need money."

"Tom left fifty dollars on the kitchen table the morning he left. It's mostly gone now, but we'll manage."

"I'm sorry if I spoke out of turn, ma'am, but I'm a questioning man by nature," Sam said. "It's a fault of old age, I guess."

Hannah smiled. "You're not old, Mr. Sawyer."

"I'm fifty."

"Oh, I thought you were—" Hannah stopped herself, horrified.

"Older?" Sam said. "I take no offense, ma'am. Cowboyin' can surely put years on a man."

"I . . . I meant . . ." Hannah began. She realized she was digging a deeper hole and gave up. "I'd better take the dishes to the sink," she said. The woman stood and picked up Sam's plate. She glanced out the cabin window and froze in place, her eyes searching outside.

"He's there again," she said.

Sam rose. "Who's there, ma'am?"

"The Apache."

Alarmed, Sam drew his Colt.

"Where is he?" he said.

"Look," Hannah said. "Out there, by the cotton-woods."

Sam stepped to the window. The day was shading into evening, and the red-streaked sky tinted the dusty air with amber light.

He made out the cottonwoods but failed to spot the Indian.

"I don't see him," he said. "My eyes ain't what they once was."

"Between the two cottonwoods to the left of the rock pile," Hannah said. "He sits a gray pony and just . . . waits."

"You've seen him before?" Sam said.

"Many times, and always by the cottonwoods."

"If you see one Injun, that means a passel of them are nearby. Does he ever come closer to the cabin?"

"No, never. He doesn't even look this way, as though the cabin doesn't exist."

"I don't see him," Sam said again. He again felt the need to apologize. "I never was a farsighted man, ma'am." He gave Hannah a wan smile. "Come to that, I'm not a close-sighted man either."

"He won't do us any harm," Hannah said. "He never has."

Lori tugged on her mother's skirt. "Is it the Indian, Mommy?"

"Yes," Hannah said. "It's the Indian." She turned and bent over the child. "Go get Dolly. It's time she was in bed."

"Dolly doesn't want to go to bed."

"Then take her on your knee and tell her a story."

"No. Pick me up. I want to see the Indian."

The Apache had Sam on edge. "You mind your ma, girl," he said.

Perhaps intimidated by a male voice, Lori said, "Nobody lets me see anything." But she walked away, accusing eyes on Sam. "I'm going to tell Dolly," she said.

Sam waited until the child was occupied with her doll. Then he said to Hannah, "Time I spoke with that Apache, tell him to move on and quit bothering white folks."

"Do you think it's wise?" the woman said.

"No, it's not wise," Sam said. "But maybe I can talk him into gettin' me my horse back."

Chapter 5

Sam Sawyer stepped out, his Colt up and ready.

Darkness didn't yet crowd him close and the cottonwoods remained visible in stark relief against a scarlet and jade sky. The desert was quiet and the hollow call of a coyote served only to make it quieter still.

Sam's eyesight had been burned out by hard years of driving herds through sun, wind, rain, and snow. Staring across the vast distances of plains that began where he was at and ended where he was yet to be had also taken its toll.

Now he saw the trees well enough, but not the Apache on the gray pony.

He'd have to get closer. A lot closer.

Sam walked on, his booted feet making little noise. Above him a hawk glided and made a *kee-kee-kee* sound as it rode the high wind currents. The hawk, a black, angular silhouette against the sky, troubled Sam, but for the life of him he didn't know why.

Then the hair rose on the back of his neck. Hell, he'd walked too far. The Indian was behind him on his right, not ten yards away. The Apache sat his pony under an ancient, spreading oak that had no right to be there.

Sam turned and said, "Stay right where you're at, Injun." He fought to keep his voice calm. "I can drill you dead center from here."

Now he was near enough to the Apache to notice a couple of things: The man was painted for war and he sat his horse as still as a statue of a Civil War general in a town square. The Apache remained motionless and didn't glance in Sam's direction.

All right, Sam decided, maybe the Indian couldn't understand good ol' American.

He thumbed back the hammer of his Colt, the triple click loud in the silence, and said, "*Bajese de su caballo o yo le matare.*" His threat in Mexican to shoot the Apache off his horse didn't work either.

The warrior stayed where he was, his eyes fixed on a distance Sam couldn't see, man and horse an unmoving pillar of alabaster in the mother-of-pearl dusk.

His confidence waning as fast as the light, Sam grew desperate. His chin jutting, he stepped toward the Apache. "All right, we'll play it your way," he said. "I'm pulling you off'n that danged pony."

The Indian's horse tossed its head, then moved forward at an unhurried walk. Then the hawk dived low, its talons raking the top of Sam's hat. Cussing, Sam waved off the swooping hawk, then took a step to the side and let the horse and rider pass.

The Apache didn't look at him, his lusterless black eyes fixed on an invisible horizon many miles distant.

It was then that Sam saw a bullet hole in the middle of the warrior's forehead, crusted with dried-black blood. His breath stilled in his chest, Sam's eyes widened and he felt fear like ice water in his belly.

As the Apache rode past, his pony's hooves making no sound, Sam smelled sage and pine . . . and something else . . . something he half remembered . . . the sweet, acrid stench of a decaying body.

The American cowboy was, and remains, the most superstitious creature on earth, and Sam had all the puncher's inborn fears of ha'nts and ghosts and shadowed places where eyes glow in the gloom like sparks of fire.

He watched the Apache clear the trees and slowly melt into the dim hall of the night so that no trace of man or horse remained. Then, as fast as bad knees and aching feet allowed, Sam turned and sprinted for the cabin, as scared as he'd ever been in his life.

Hannah met Sam at the door, the shotgun in her hands. "What happened?" she said. "I heard you running."

"I wanted to make sure you were all right," Sam said, blinking. His breath came in shallow, quick gasps.

"The Apache?" Hannah said.

"I moved him on."

Hannah lowered the Greener. Her eyes sought Sam's in the darkness, probing with that uncanny ability a woman has that tells her when a man is lying. "Now let me know what really happened," she said.

"Are we going to talk all night on the

doorstep?" Sam said, glancing quickly over his shoulder.

"Come in," Hannah said. "The coffee is still hot."

She waited until Sam drank coffee and built his second cigarette with unsteady hands. Then she said, "I didn't hear a gunshot. I didn't hear anything, though I thought I heard the cry of a hawk."

Sam shook his head. "No, there was no shooting and danged little talking."

A silence stretched between them, grew taut.

"What happened, Sam?" Hannah said finally.

It was the first time the woman had used his given name, and Sam took pleasure in it. But it was a long time before he answered. Then he said, "The Apache is riding a different trail from the rest of us." He sought a way to express himself, then: "I reckon he's looking for a place where only dead Indians go."

He saw the confused expression on the woman's face, the crease that appeared between her eyes.

"Where's Lori?" he said.

"Asleep. She and Dolly dozed off in the chair."

"The Apache is dead, Hannah."

"You killed him?"

"Somebody killed him, but it wasn't me. And it was a long time ago."

"Sam, I don't understand."

"Like I said, the Injun's been dead for a long time."

"But how . . . I mean . . ."

"Hannah, he ain't a living man and he ain't a dead one either."

"A ghost? Do you mean he's a ghost?"

"Something like that." Sam drew deep on his cigarette. "Call him what you want, but he ain't alive no more."

"How do you know?"

"Do you want me to draw you a picture?"

"How do you know?"

Sam pointed to the middle of his forehead. "He's got a bullet hole right there, and it happened months, maybe years ago."

Hannah sat in stunned silence for a few moments, then said, "Is it an omen?"

"Could be," Sam said. "But is it a good omen or a bad one? And who is it for? It ain't for me or you. Leastways, I don't think so."

Hannah didn't answer. Finally she crossed her arms and rubbed her shoulders and said, "Gosh, all of a sudden it's cold in here."

"Yeah, it sure is," Sam said. "All of a sudden."

A moment later someone hammered on the cabin door.

Chapter 6

Startled, Sam Sawyer jumped to his feet and drew his Colt. He put a finger to his lips and hushed Hannah into silence, then stepped to the door.

"Who's there?" Sam said, his mouth to the door's rough timber. "I warn you, I ain't sittin' on my gun hand here, so if'n you're a dead Injun, you're gonna be a sight deader."

There was a moment's silence. Then a man's voice said, "I'm an honest traveler, seeking food and shelter."

"What are you doing out there at this time of night?" Sam said. He was aware that Hannah had taken down her shotgun and had stepped into shadow.

"I'm afraid I've lost my way," the man outside said.

"Where you from, mister?" Sam said.

"Silver City. I was headed for a town called Lost Mine, but I seem to have mislaid the place."

"It's south of here," Sam said.

"Yes, but can I find it in this Stygian gloom?"

Sam thumbed back the hammer of his revolver, the triple click loud in the silence. "State your intentions," he said.

"As I said earlier, I seek shelter for the night and perhaps a light repast. I mean, if that's not too much trouble."

"Hell, it is too—"

"Sam, let him in," Hannah said.

"You sure?" Sam said. "He might be another dead Injun."

Hannah smiled. "I'm sure he's not."

Sam spoke through the door again. "What's your name, mister? An' don't say Sittin' Bull or I'll shoot ya."

"My name is Jasper Perry, of the Oldham County, Texas, Perrys."

"Are you a true-blue white man?" Sam said.

"I'm the product of ten centuries of Anglo-Saxon inbreeding, yes."

"Please let the gentleman in, Sam," Hannah said. "It's getting cold out."

Sam lifted the latch on the door and opened it wide. "All right, come inside," he said.

And all seven feet of Jasper Perry walked into the cabin, bending low to clear the top of the doorway.

He saw Hannah immediately and doffed his top hat. "Thank you for your hospitality, ma'am," he said. "There's a most singular strangeness in the night that's greatly disturbing."

"See any dead Apaches, pilgrim?" Sam said, refusing to be friendly.

"No." Perry smiled, his teeth as long and

39

yellow as piano keys. "But they might well be out there."

"Can I get you a cup of coffee, Mr. Perry?" Hannah said.

"That would be much appreciated," Perry said, smiling again.

The tall man was dressed in a claw-hammer black coat and tight pants of the same shade. He wore a boiled white shirt with a four-in-hand tie and elastic-sided boots.

"Sam, would you fetch a chair from the table for Mr. Perry and put it close to the fire," Hannah said.

Sam studied the man from the soles of his shoes to the top of his bald head and said, "Can you sit in a chair for normal folks?"

"I'm sure I can manage, Mr. . . . uh . . ."

"Sawyer, as ever was," Sam said.

Perry folded his lanky body into a sitting position on the chair and said, "Much obliged, Mr. Sawyer." He spread his long, thin hands to the fire. "This is indeed cozy," he said.

Sam doubted that Perry was comfortable, on account of how his bent knees were level with his shoulders, but the man seemed at ease, as though he were in his own home.

And that irritated Sam.

"State your business in Lost Mine," he said.

Perry took time to accept coffee from Hannah and smile his thanks before he answered, "I'm to hang three men there at three o'clock sharp tomorrow afternoon."

"Are you some kind of a lawman?" Sam said.

"No, Mr. Sawyer, I'm a hangman. That is my profession."

Even to a talking man like Sam, that statement was a conversation stopper, and he sat staring at Perry in what he would later describe as "a strangled silence."

Hannah recovered from her shock more quickly. "Lost Mine is Sheriff Vic Moseley's town," she said. "He's a . . . friend of mine."

"And that is the very gentlemen who summoned me by wire," Perry said. "He stated that his last hanging was bungled and this time he wanted a professional job done of it."

"Don't take much training to hang a man," Sam said, scowling. He was irritated at Hannah's mention of Vic Moseley.

"Oh, but you're wrong, Mr. Sawyer," Perry said. He laid his cup by his side and clasped his bony knees as he warmed to his subject. "It's the drop, you see."

"You mean you need to get the drop on a man afore you string him up?" Sam said.

"Oh dear, no," Perry said. "After the gallows trapdoor opens, the drop is how far the condemned must fall before the noose tightens and breaks his neck."

If Perry heard Hannah's sharp intake of breath

and the quickening pace of her knitting needles, he ignored it.

"Now," he said, "the distance of the drop depends on a man's weight, and, yes, his height." The hangman fished in an inside pocket and produced a scrap of paper. "This is a follow-up wire I requested from Sheriff Moseley." He settled a pair of pince-nez glasses at the end of his long, bony nose, scanned the wire, and said, "Yes . . . Now, where are we? Ah yes, here it is, the condemned are as follows . . .

" 'Key Felts, white, aged thirty-six, height five foot six, weight one hundred and thirty pounds.' "

Perry paused for effect, then read, " 'Isaiah Walker, Negro, aged nineteen, height five foot ten, weight one hundred and seventy pounds.

" 'And Lucius Noftsinger, white, age unknown, height five foot seven, weight one hundred and twenty pounds.' "

Hannah rose and refilled Perry's cup, and the hangman nodded his thanks. "So you see, Mr. Sawyer," he said, "the differences in the weight and stature of the condemned means that I must calculate a different drop for each one. That"—Perry smiled—"is where my professional expertise comes in. We don't want to bungle the thing and tear the condemned's head off, now, do we?"

Sam opened his mouth to speak, but Hannah got there before he did. "I suppose the three men are murderers, Mr. Perry?" she said. "And that's why Vic, I mean Sheriff Moseley, is hanging them."

"Bless your heart, ma'am, no," the hangman said. "All three are petty thieves, drunks, and dance hall loungers. In his wire, the sheriff calls them 'damned nuisances.' That's rather funny in a way."

Hannah looked stricken. "Mr. Perry, I can't believe that Vic would hang men for so little reason. Surely you're mistaken."

The hangman shook his head. "No mistake, ma'am." He held the wire out to Hannah, pointed at it with a thin forefinger, and said, "See, down there. All three are described as petty thieves."

"That ain't much reason to hang a man," Sam said.

"I assume that a circuit judge thought differently," Perry said.

Hannah shook her head. "I can't believe it. I won't believe it. There must be something else. There's only so much Vic could explain to you in a wire."

"Perhaps, ma'am," Perry said. "But when I report to the United States Marshal in Silver City, I will give the reason for the executions as petty thievery."

"Mr. Perry, Vic Moseley is a fine man and an upstanding law officer," Hannah said. "I can't believe he'd be a party to a . . . a judicial murder."

The hangman sat in thought for a few moments, then said, "If it's any consolation, ma'am, a sheriff's duty is to carry out the commands of the court. He does not sit in judgment."

"Then that must be the case," Hannah said. "Vic would not condemn three men for such trifling crimes."

"Indeed, ma'am," Perry said. "That must be the case indeed."

But the hangman's voice carried little conviction, a thing Sam Sawyer noticed but Hannah didn't.

Chapter 7

Sam Sawyer and Jasper Perry slept on the cabin floor that night. Hannah, upset by all the talk about dead Apaches and hangings, insisted that the barn had lain empty for a long time and was full of rats. In reality she needed the company of men close by.

"I'll give you each a blanket and a pillow," she'd said. "They're clean and you'll be warm enough."

"Suits me just fine, ma'am," Sam said. "I've slept in a lot worse places."

He was glad of the offer. Spooked by the dead Apache and the presence of a hangman, he needed the woman close.

Come morning after breakfast, Perry mounted his mule and headed for Lost Mine. After the hangman was gone, Sam began to take his leave of Hannah Stewart and her daughter.

"I reckon I'll head fer Lost Mine my own self," he said, "and see if I can find some temporary work. I'm pretty much down on my uppers."

"You'll be in time for the hangings," Hannah said, her voice flat.

"I seen a hanging once afore, Hannah, a rustler up in the Spur Lake Basin country," Sam said. "I ain't much inclined to see another."

"There's a restaurant in town, but I think it already has a cook," Hannah said.

"Well, I'll jes' have to see how the pickle squirts, like," Sam said. "Sometimes a man can see his trail ahead real clear. Sometimes he can't."

The woman stretched out her hand. "It was real nice to meet you, Sam."

Sam took the proffered hand. "And you too, Hannah."

"Don't be a stranger, now, you hear? Stop by sometime. There's always coffee in the pot."

"I surely will," Sam said. "And give my regards to the little one when she wakes. She's going to break hearts one day."

"Take care, Sam."

"And you too, Hannah. An' don't worry none about that Injun. He don't mean any harm."

Sam walked away from the cabin toward the rise. The morning light was fresh and clear as the new day came in bright, and birds sang in the piñon trees.

"Sam!"

He turned and saw Hannah at the cabin door.

"You will come back and see us, now," she said. "Set for a spell."

Sam waved, smiled, and walked on.

He had nothing to say because he didn't know how he felt, about Hannah, about anything.

"Good beer," Sam Sawyer said. "Nice and cold."

"Enjoy it while you can," the bartender said. "The winter ice is all but gone."

Outside, dust devils danced along Lost Mine's only street, a wide enough thoroughfare book-ended by a row of buildings on the east side, only four to the west, a livery stable, a warehouse, a barbershop, and the Lone Star Saloon. Stock corrals marked the southern limit of the town, and near those a huddle of small shacks where the girls who worked the line lived when the drovers were in town.

But the morning Sam walked into town, Lost Mine was saved from dusty drabness by a new gallows, hung with red, white, and blue bunting. The platform was large enough to accommodate the three men who were due to be hanged that afternoon, plus the hangman, the preacher, the sheriff, and a few other officials. Nearby, with slack-mouthed patience, a Mexican boy turned a pig on a spit, and behind him a couple of barrels of beer had been set up on a table.

"Here for the hanging?" the bartender asked, wiping the counter in front of Sam.

"Nah, looking for work," Sam said. "But only temporary-like. I'm headed for Silver City."

"Silver City is the place to find work," said the bartender, a magnificent creature with slicked-down hair, parted in the middle, a brocaded vest, and a diamond stickpin in his cravat. "No work around here, though," he said. And then because he was bored: "You lookin' to sign on with a cattle outfit?"

"Too old an' busted up for that anymore," Sam said. "I thought I might prosper in the restaurant profession."

"The only restaurant in town is the Cupboard, but the owner does all the cooking. If you can call it that."

The only other customer in the saloon was a big, yellow-haired man who'd been sitting at a table, drinking coffee from a china cup. Now he rose and stepped outside, and the bartender said, "That there was Sheriff Moseley. He'll be officiating at the hanging."

"Is that a fact?" Sam said.

"Yeah, it's a fact. He's done it before, so folks expect this'n will go without a hitch." The bartender lit his morning cigar and said behind a cloud of curling blue smoke, "Of course, it all depends on the three rannies getting hung, you understand."

"Yeah, I guess it would at that," Sam said. He passed his glass to the bartender. "Fill 'er up again."

"On the house," the bartender said as he thumped the beer on the counter. "On account of how your poke is a might shy on ballast and I went up the trail myself back in the day."

"I'm obliged," Sam said. Then, because he was a talking man and mildly curious: "How can them three rannies make it a good hangin' for the folks?"

"Well, mister, we got a pig out there and two barrels of beer, all provided by the mayor and the city council," the bartender said. He had a gold tooth that glinted when he spoke.

"I smell that hog," Sam said.

"Depend on it, so do the folks around town," the bartender said. "But if they're getting free pig meat and beer, they need time to enjoy it. You catching my drift?"

Sam shook his head. "No, I sure ain't."

"They need speechifying to draw the celebration out," the bartender said. "And that's where the rannies who're getting hung come in. The womenfolk expect a speech from the condemned, the one about how strong drink and loose women brought them to this pass, even though they had a good mother." The bartender nodded. "That bit about mother always pleases the females. Hell, there won't be a dry eye in the crowd."

A couple of businessmen in broadcloth stepped into the saloon, and as he stepped away to serve them, the bartender said to Sam, "If you're sharp set, help yourself to the cheese at the end of the bar and there's soda crackers in the barrel."

The walk from Hannah Stewart's cabin had given Sam an appetite, and he ate his share of cheese and crackers before he waved to the bartender and left the saloon.

There was a rocker on the porch outside and Sam sat and built and smoked a cigarette as he watched the early crowd that had gathered around the gallows. It seemed that the pig wasn't yet cooked enough, but men were already drinking beer and women carried picnic baskets and chatted with each other, their bonneted heads nodding. The sky was blue as far as the eye could see and there was just enough breeze to take the edge off the noonday heat. Sam figured it was a perfect day for a hanging.

Boots sounded on the timber boards to his left, and Sam turned and saw Sheriff Vic Moseley stride toward him.

"Howdy there, stranger," he said. "I heard you say in the saloon you're seeking employment."

"I sure am," Sam said, smiling, prepared to be sociable. "Apaches took my hoss an' saddle and

I'm down to the eight dollars in my jeans." Sam eyed the star pinned to the man's shirt under his canvas vest. "You must be Sheriff Vic Moseley," he said.

"That would be me," the man said. "And who do I have the pleasure of addressing?"

Sam gave his name, then said, "Out of the Spur Lake Basin country, an' before that Uvalde County, Texas."

"How did you know my name?" Moseley said.

"Stayed the night at a cabin just north of here," Sam said. "Gal by the name of Hannah Stewart told me you visited by times."

"A fine-looking woman, Miz Hannah," the sheriff said, his eyes speculative.

Sam nodded. "Yep, she's all of that."

"Me and Hannah have an understanding," Moseley said. "One day I plan to take her as my wife and bed her."

"You could do worse," Sam said.

The sheriff considered that and seemed satisfied he was not facing a rival. Moseley was a tall, handsome man with the intolerant, hard face and harder eyes of a Salem witch-burner.

To Sam, he didn't look like a gunfighter, more of a cow town politician who preferred to count votes rather than the notches on his gun.

But he looked big enough and mean enough to be a handful in any kind of scrape. Sam had no doubt on that score.

Moseley waited until Sam lit another cigarette, then said, "I'm a blunt-talking man, so I'll come right to the point. How would you like to make twenty dollars?"

"I'd like that just fine," Sam said. "What do I have to do?"

The sheriff didn't hesitate. "I want you to mend the broken heart of a little girl."

"Mending womenfolk's broken hearts is a tad out of my line," Sam said, taken aback. "The fact is, I never could trust a man who can look a pretty woman in the eye."

"You'd be doing a service to the girl's parents, this town, and me personally," Moseley said. "I'd be mighty grateful enough that I'd help you find that restaurant job you want." He puffed up a little. "I have friends in Silver City, you know. Powerful friends."

Sam needed the twenty dollars, and after his initial shock he wasn't about to talk himself out of it.

"What do I have to do to mend the kid's broken heart?" he said. Then, his jocular mood aided by the second beer, he said, "Shoot her?"

Moseley's smile was wintry. "No, nothing as drastic as that. I'll let her father explain all to you. His name is Mr. Jerome T. Meriwether and he's the right honorable mayor of this fair town."

"Well," Sam said, getting to his feet, "I'm ready to meet the gentleman."

Moseley shook his head. "Slow down, pardner. I'll take you to him after the hangings."

Sam sat again. "Suits me, Sheriff."

"Go over there and get yourself some roast pig and a beer," Moseley said. "As soon as the three criminals are bedded down, I'll introduce you to His Honor."

Without another word the sheriff stepped off the porch and headed toward the jailhouse, his walk long striding and arrogant. Sam watched the man go and felt a shiver, as though a dark shadow had fallen over him.

Chapter 8

The local newspaper, a single sheet published three days after the hangings, summed up why Sheriff Vic Moseley was not popular with the crowd who blamed him for the event's low entertainment value.

THREE MEN
HURLED INTO ETERNITY
IN A MOMENT

One Man's Last Words: "Go to H—"
Necks Cleanly Broken, Says Hangman
Roast Pig Undercooked
Sheriff Moseley Blamed for Uneatable Hog

But both the hangings and the headlines were yet to come when Sam Sawyer strolled over to the gallows and poured himself a beer from one of the barrels.

Jasper Perry was already on the gallows, testing the three ropes to make sure the hemp hadn't been stretched. When he saw Sam he hopped down the steps like a great black crow and shook his hand warmly.

"Mr. Sawyer, how nice of you to come," he said. "Is the fair Mrs. Stewart with you?"

"No," Sam said, "I came by myself."

"A great day, Mr. Sawyer," Perry said. "I would say a most singular day that's of the greatest moment."

"Indeed, it is, Mr. Perry," Sam said, wishing that the hangman would get back on the gallows where he belonged.

"Good drops and clean breaks, that's what you'll see today," Perry said. "My professional pride would have it no other way."

A woman in the crowd yelled, "Hey, Mr. Hangman, is it true that one of them boys wore the gray?"

"Set your mind at rest, dear lady," Perry said. "None of the miscreants served our noble cause."

"I'm a Yankee and proud of it," the woman said, and flounced away.

"Sadly, in my profession, you just can't please everybody, Mr. Sawyer," Perry said, watching the woman go. "Even the condemned can be demanding."

"I hear there will be speechifying afore the drop," Sam said.

"Yes, there always is," said Perry. "Sometimes a condemned man can be quite eloquent when he speaks of ardent spirits"—he smiled—"and even more ardent women."

The hangman laid his cold, bony hand on Sam's shoulder and said, "I must get back to work, but I set store by your opinion, Mr. Sawyer, so later please tell me what you think of my work. It is an art, you know."

Sam nodded. "I surely will," he said, but he'd no intention of watching the hangings or ever seeing Jasper Perry again.

"Hell, did you watch the hangings?" Vic Moseley said.

Sam shook his head. "No, I didn't."

"You didn't miss much. The thing was over before it began, so the blasted pig was raw and I got the blame for that as well as the no speechifying," Moseley said.

"Well, you're the biggest toad in the puddle, Sheriff," Sam said.

Moseley might've taken offense at that remark, but he was venting his spleen, not listening.

"I gave them boys a bottle of whiskey and they promised to put on a good show," the sheriff said. "What did I get? A 'go to hell,' that's what I got."

"Just don't seem right," Sam said. "Them takin' a man's whiskey under false pretenses an' all."

"You bet it ain't right. If I could string up them three again, I would. And this time I'd make it last. Danged hangman should've known you don't stretch a man's neck that fast."

For a moment Moseley stared at Sam as though he were the source of all his troubles. But then he sighed and said, "Let's go see the mayor."

The mayor's combined dwelling and office was the only redbrick structure in town, a low building that had a shady porch out front lined with white wicker rocking chairs. Behind was a barn, a smokehouse, and other outbuildings.

Sheriff Moseley told Sam to wait on the porch. Then he opened the door and stepped inside. He was gone a long time, so long that Sam reckoned the lawman had forgotten about him. But Moseley eventually opened the door and stuck his head outside. "Come in, Mr. . . . uh . . . uh . . ."

"Sawyer," Sam said.

"Yes," the sheriff said, "of course you are. Please come in. The mayor is ready to see you now."

Mayor Jerome T. Meriwether was a small, thin

man with the furtive, shifty-eyed look of the henpecked husband. He wore a frock coat of gray broadcloth and a collarless shirt, and he studied Sam with sad, wounded eyes. A Remington revolver with a bone handle lay on the desk in front of him.

He offered no greeting, just a raspy "Has Sheriff Moseley told you what you must do to earn your twenty dollars?"

Sam hesitated a moment to collect his thoughts.

"Come, now, man," Meriwether said. "Be brief. A simple yes or no will do. I don't have time for dillydally, shilly-shally. You heard about the hangings? A sham, a blasted sham, and a bloody shame. Now speak up."

"The sheriff said he wants me to mend a little girl's broken heart," Sam said.

"And that's all? Come, man, let's hear it."

"Yes. I reckon that's about all."

The mayor gave Moseley an irritated look. "Why does it take Texans half the day to say five or six words?"

The sheriff said nothing, and Meriwether shook his head. "It's a heathen way of talking."

Sam decided he didn't like the mayor. The man had the look of a Yankee carpetbagger, the worst of the plundering flotsam and jetsam thrown up on Southern shores after the War Between the States. But Sam was here to earn twenty dollars, not to measure the man, so he kept his mouth shut.

"Five days ago," Meriwether said, "in this very town, Dale Johansson's dry goods store was robbed of thirty-seven dollars and eighteen cents and a jar of stick candy. On the way out of town, the miscreants stole my daughter's skewbald pony from my barn." The mayor leaned across his desk. "Do you follow me so far?"

"I reckon I do," Sam said.

"Good. Then you're not quite as lost as you look."

"I always know where I'm at," Sam said.

Meriwether ignored that and said, "Soon you will behold a piteous sight, Mr. . . . uh . . ."

"Sawyer," Sam said.

"Yes, indeed, Mr. Sawyer." The mayor held a handkerchief to his nose and blew loudly. When he finished wiping and returned the cloth to his pocket, he said, "I will take you to meet my daughter. She's only twelve, a mere child, and she's heartbroken. She wants her pony back, and I'm hiring you to get it for her."

"Whoa, Mayor," Sam said, "don't hang the gate until the corral's built. I don't want to be rushing into things here. Who was the ranny who took the hoss, and will he be willing to give it back?"

"You may have to persuade him," Sheriff Moseley said.

"You mean gun persuadin'?" Sam said.

"Yes, if need be," Meriwether said.

Sam took time to get his thoughts in order. When he did, he said, "Mayor, the only thing I ever used my iron for was to string bobwire fence an' lately to take pots at thieving Apaches that I missed every time." He shook his head. "I'm no gun hand."

A series of high-pitched, wailing screeches raked across the fabric of the morning silence like talons. Sam glanced out the window. The few people walking in the street had frozen in their tracks, looking beyond the mayor's office to the houses beyond.

"What," Sam said, "in the world is that?"

"My daughter giving voice to her grief," Meriwether said. "Soon you will meet her and share in her anguish."

"Mayor, I've been thinking, and I reckon I don't need the twenty dollars that badly," Sam said. "I guess I'll be moving on."

"Wait," Meriwether said. "Sheriff Moseley says you have no horse. It's a long walk from here to Silver City, especially with the Apaches out."

"I'm listening," Sam said. "Have you got something more to say, add to the pot, like?"

"Yes, and here it is. In addition to the twenty dollars, I'll supply you with a saddled mount. When you bring the skewbald pony back, the horse will be yours." It was a bad mistake for the mayor to smile. It made him look like a grinning rattlesnake. "Now, what do you say, Mr. . . . uh . . . ? Speak up, fellow."

Sam would not be pushed. "Hold on there just a minute," he said. "By nature I'm a questioning man."

"Then ask your questions," the mayor said. "I'm a busy man."

"How come the sheriff ain't going after the skewbald pony?" Sam said.

"Good question." Moseley beamed. He looked at Meriwether. "Is that not a good question, Your Honor?"

"Answer it, then, for goodness' sake," the mayor said, irritated. He winced as more prolonged screams echoed around the town like fingernails on a chalkboard.

"I say the recovery of the pony is a county matter," Moseley said, raising his voice above the din. "The county sheriff says it's a town matter. But he also says I have no county jurisdiction, so you see how it is with me."

"No, I don't," Sam said.

"My hands are tied. If I have no jurisdiction outside the town limits, I can't get the skewbald pony back. And if I attempt it . . . well, the county sheriff would love to find an excuse to arrest me and strip me of my office."

"So it's down to you, Mr. . . . uh . . ." the mayor said.

Sam smelled a rat. The fact is, he smelled a passel of them.

"You didn't tell me this afore," he said, "but who was the ranny who stole the pony in the first place?"

Moseley and the mayor exchanged glances. Then the sheriff said in a small voice, "Dan Wells and his three brothers."

Sam Sawyer almost fainted and had to lean on the mayor's desk to steady himself.

Chapter 9

"Here, drink this," the mayor said, handing Sam the glass of water he'd just poured from the pitcher on his desk. "You took a turn."

Sam drank the water, then set the glass on the desk with a thud.

"Are you talking about Starvin' Dan Wells, the feller who ate the Comanche in Fannin County, Texas, a few years back?" he said.

"He didn't eat a whole Comanche," Sheriff Moseley said. "That story gets exaggerated every time it's told."

"He only ate the Indian's liver and heart," Meriwether said. "A snack, you might call it."

"Why did he do that?" Sam said, horrified.

"Because he said he always wanted to know what a Comanche tasted like," Moseley answered.

"How the hell should I know? Wells did confess later that he regretted it, and some say he's gotten religion since."

"And that's why he robbed a store and stole a hoss," Sam said.

A silence stretched tight in the office—until it was shattered by another round of female shrieking.

"Forty dollars," the mayor said quickly. "I can't say fairer than that."

"And a horse," Moseley said. He laid a hand on Sam's shoulder. "Just Injun up on Wells's place and steal the pony back. Gunfighting don't even have to enter into it."

"Find yourself another rube," Sam said. "Summing it up fer you gents—I ain't doin' it."

"Is that your last word on the subject?" Meriwether said.

"Yep," Sam said, heading for the door. "My talkin' is done and I'm outta here."

"Sheriff Moseley, arrest that man on a charge of vagrancy," the mayor said. "He's up to no good, I'll be bound."

Moseley stepped in front of Sam, and Sam put his dukes up. But the sheriff's right hand moved with lightning speed and Sam felt the barrel of the lawman's gun slam into his head . . .

And then he felt nothing at all.

Sam Sawyer woke to a splitting headache and the taste of raw iron in his mouth. The waning afternoon sun angled through a narrow, barred window above his cot and made dust motes dance like tiny moths.

He groaned and tried to recollect what had happened.

Then he remembered: Sheriff Vic Moseley had buffaloed him. The man was faster with a gun than he'd given him credit for.

Sam touched fingertips to the side of his head. He felt a bump the size of a hen's egg, but there was no blood. A good sign, he reckoned.

For a while he lay still and watched the beam of sunlight. He heard rats rustle in a corner, and his cell smelled of piss and ancient vomit. As the light faded to darkness, the cell door opened. Sam rose to his feet and stood at the bars just as Moseley entered with a lit oil lamp.

The sheriff set the lamp on a wall bracket, then turned to look at his prisoner. "You're awake," he said.

"I'd say that's kinda obvious," Sam said. He let anger creep into his voice. "How come you buffaloed me and how long do you plan to keep me here?"

Moseley smiled. "Answer to the first question—because you resisted arrest. Answer to the second question—until you've paid your fine."

"What fine?"

"The one the mayor had Judge Rawlins impose

on you for vagrancy and assault on an officer of the law."

"Damn you, Moseley, how big a fine?"

"Twenty-five dollars."

"How am I gonna come up with twenty-five dollars?"

"I don't rightly know," the sheriff said. "Do you have any friends or kinfolk around that might spring for the money?"

"You know I don't."

"Then you're in for a long visit, ain't you?" Moseley smiled, his teeth white under his groomed mustache. "By the way, I took the eight dollars you had in your pocket. It'll help pay for your grub until you come up with the fine."

"You go to hell," Sam said. "You're a danged robber."

Moseley ignored that and said, "The menu for tonight is beans and warmed-over coffee. Of course, the menu for every night is beans and warmed-over coffee."

The lamp cast a dull orange glow, enough for Sam to see for the first time the man in the next cell who stood at the dividing bars, watching him.

Startled, Sam said, "I didn't see you there afore."

"I was lying on my bunk"—the man pointed into the shadows—"there."

"What you in for?" Sam said, prepared as always to be sociable.

"Public drunkenness," the man said.

Sam blinked against the gloom. "You know, at first I took ye fer an Injun."

"I am an Injun," the man said. "Kiowa. Black Crow's band."

Sam extended his hand and the Indian took it.

"Name's Sam Sawyer, down from Spur Lake Basin way."

"Call me James," the Kiowa said. "Down from nowhere."

"When do you get out?" Sam said. "You seem sober enough."

The Indian was a small man with a great beak of a nose and a wide, narrow mouth. His black hair hung over his narrow shoulders in two thick braids and he wore a white man's coat and flat-brimmed hat.

"I get out soon," James said. "I go with you."

Sam's laugh was thin. "Then you'll be a long time a-waiting. I can't get out until I pay twenty-five dollars I don't have."

"I go with you," the Kiowa said. "Sheriff Moseley say so."

"I'm not catching your drift," Sam said.

"I help you return the skewbald pony. We go to the cabin of Dan Wells, the Injun-eater, and steal back the skewbald hoss." James thumped his chest with his fist. "Kiowa good hoss thieves. Everybody say so."

Sam's anger flared, directed at Moseley, not

the Indian. "What did that no-good tinhorn of a sheriff promise you?"

"He promise me nothing," James said. "He only say that if I don't go, something mighty bad will happen to my wife and daughter."

"But he can't do that," Sam said. "It's agin' the law."

"White man's law don't stretch to Indians," James said. "Bad thing, but there it is."

"Dang Moseley's eyes," Sam said. "That . . . that—" He couldn't find the words to express his feelings, and said instead, "Where is your missus and the kid?"

"Live in shack, edge of town. Good Lipan Apache woman."

Sam figured out Moseley's angle, and his anger grew. "Here's how I figure it. The sheriff is scared to go anywhere near Dan Wells and his cannibal clan. That much is obvious. Even to me."

The Kiowa grunted his agreement. "Maybe so," he said.

"But he figures that if he gives me forty dollars and a hoss, I'll keep on riding. And he's right about that."

Sam stabbed a forefinger at the Kiowa. "You're Moseley's ace in the hole. He reckons you'll keep an eye on me and stop me from making the big skedaddle. Well, that's what he figures anyway."

James clenched both hands to the bars and pushed his face closer to Sam.

"Sheriff Moseley likes to hurt women," he said. "He beat up a girl three months ago and the town covered it up. She was only a Mexican girl working the line and nobody cared. But I did care. She was nice to me, gave me whiskey and a dress for my wife." The Kiowa reached out and grabbed Sam by the front of his shirt. "Listen to me. If we don't come back with the skewbald pony, Moseley will murder my wife and daughter. I will not let that happen."

"When you get out of here, why don't you gun him down?" Sam said.

"No good, Sammy. Sheriff is very fast with a gun. The only way I can beat him is shoot him in the back. Then I'll be hung for sure, and what happens to my wife and daughter then?" James waited a heartbeat, then said, "My wife and my child will starve."

"Tarnation, James," Sam said, "I'm mad at you. You've made me look at myself, like you was a mirror of my soul, and all of a sudden I don't like what I see."

He turned away from the Kiowa and stepped to the front bars of the cell. "Moseley, you buzzard, come here!" he yelled. "I want to talk to you."

Chapter 10

"You ever seen an uglier kid in all your born days?" Sam Sawyer said.

"Fat," James said. "She had the eyes of a pig."

"And she could squeal like a pig, couldn't she? Her face got red as a trail cook's fire, and with all them yellow ringlets, man, it was a sight to see."

"She kicked you," the Kiowa said. "Then kicked her ma and her pa."

"Yeah, I know. I still have the bruise on my shin."

"She wanted the sheriff to go after her pony, not an Injun and an old man."

"I'm not an old man."

"Girl said you were, not me."

"She said you was a no-good, drunken, skinny redskin."

"Well, she was right about that," James said. He nodded ahead of him. "River coming up, Sammy."

A few minutes later they crossed the Gila River where it branched west toward Black Mountain and the Arizona border, then rode through the still morning, the mountains of the Pinos Altos Range rising to their east, their peaks gilded by the first rays of the rising sun.

The air smelled of pine and summer wild-flowers and the day was not yet hot. It was a morning for a courting couple to hold hands and look at the sky and whisper words tied into love knots.

"Dang saddle is scouring my rear," Sam said, grimacing as he shifted his weight.

"McClellan saddle was made to favor the hoss," James said.

"How do you know that?"

"Soldier tell me that one time. I don't remember when."

The Kiowa rode bareback on a swaybacked paint that was probably worth five dollars for its tallow and hide. Sam's mount wasn't much better, a hammerheaded mustang with a punishing gait, a mean eye, and a wheeze.

Sam nodded to the battered Sharps .50 the Kiowa carried across the withers of his pony. "You any good with that?"

"Nope." The Indian touched the butt of Sam's Colt. "You any good with that?"

"Nope."

The Kiowa nodded, but said nothing, his face like stone.

"Up on the Spur Lake Basin, I heard men talk about Dan Wells and his brothers," Sam said after a while. "They say them boys can skin iron quicker'n scat and hit what they're aiming at."

"The Injun-eater has killed many men," James said. "Both white and red. He is good with the gun."

"Then what are we doing here?"

"We're going to bring back the skewbald pony," the Kiowa said.

"Well, we ain't got it yet," Sam said. Then, his irritation growing, he said, "How come a Kiowa don't know how to shoot a rifle gun? Every Injun I ever knew could draw a bead real good."

"I never could get the hang of it," James said.

"How about a bow an' arrow?"

"Never could get the hang of that either."

"Then we're in trouble," Sam said.

The Kiowa drew rein and pointed to a forested peak to his southwest.

"That is McClure Mountain," he said. "The one Sheriff Moseley spoke of."

"Well, we swing northeast here," Sam said. Then, depression settling on his shoulders like a black raven, he said, "Not that it matters. We're both gonna die anyway."

The Kiowa smiled for the first time since Sam had met him.

"I am not a great warrior like Satanta or Big Bow," he said, "but I know how to steal a hoss."

Sam's shortsighted gaze scanned the rugged terrain of the Pinos Altos. What he saw was mostly a blur of blue and dark green, the white sky lying on top like frosting on a cake. In other words, he saw nothing at all.

As though reading Sam's mind, James said, "Moseley says there is a canyon beyond the hills where Wells has his dugout."

"A dugout is gonna be hard to find in this wilderness," Sam said, aware that he sounded like a grumpy old man.

"I've heard of the place," the Kiowa said. "His dugout sits on a rock ledge above the Gila and he has more, a saloon, a store, and a house for his women."

He turned in his saddle and looked at Sam. "Miners go there, I'm told, and sometimes Apaches."

"Apaches?" Sam said, surprised.

"They trade Mexican women for rifles and cartridges. But not all the Mescalero do this. Some fear Wells because he is an Injun-eater."

"James," Sam said, "have you given any thought to how dangerous this is gonna be? I mean, getting the skewbald pony back."

"I think only of my wife and daughter and I know what I have to do."

"All right, then let me be scared for both of us, huh?"

Chapter 11

Sam and the Kiowa rode into the timbered Pinos Altos Range as the sun began its morning climb. The highest peaks soared more than eight thousand feet above the flat and formed part of the rugged backbone of the Continental Divide. The cedar and piñon of the lower slopes gradually gave way to stands of aspen and ponderosa pine, and higher still grew stands of juniper and fir.

James topped a brush-covered hogback rise ahead of Sam and drew rein, his gaze fixed intently on the valley floor below.

"What do you see?" Sam said, stopping alongside the Kiowa.

"White men. And a woman." The Indian leaned forward in his saddle, the corners of his black eyes wrinkling. "Two women. No, one is a child."

Sam followed James's stare. "Can you make them out?"

"Who?"

"Don't be so contrary," Sam said. "All of them."

James stood on his dignity. "Even for a Kiowa, the distance is far."

He swung out of the saddle and scrambled about fifty feet lower down the slope.

"Yellow-haired woman with a child," he said, turning his head to Sam. "Two big men riding tall horses."

"I can't make out a thing," Sam said.

"Yes, far away for a close-seeing man to see," the Kiowa said, much to his companion's irritation.

James climbed back up the rise and stepped into the leather.

"One man's wife and daughter, maybe so," he said. "Or men have traded with Apaches for a woman and child."

Sam felt a spike of anxiety, but then shook his head.

Nah, it couldn't be. . . .

Then he remembered the dead Indian. An omen, Hannah Stewart had said.

Was it Hannah and Lori down in the valley? Were they captives?

"Oh my gosh, that's not two of the Wells brothers, is it?" Sam said.

The Kiowa angled him a "how the hell should I know?" look, but said only, "Maybe so, Sammy."

After a few moments' thought, Sam said, "We'll trail them. If they're Wells brothers, they'll lead us right to their dugout. If they turn out to be honest travelers, well, no harm done."

"Why your interest in the riders?" the Kiowa said.

"The yeller-haired woman might be somebody I know." He hesitated a moment, then said, "And would admire to know better."

"Then we both will fight for our woman."

"She ain't my woman," Sam said. "At least, not yet she ain't."

"Sheriff Moseley has woman with yellow hair," James said. "Could the one down yonder be the same?"

"She could be."

The Kiowa nodded. "So you want Moseley's woman, Sammy. Now he will kill you for sure."

After the riders had cleared the flat, the Kiowa led Sam down from the high country. The sun was well up in a burned-out sky and the day was hot. A persistent bee buzzed around Sam's head, and only an annoyed glance from James stopped his cussing and slapping.

"They are not far ahead of us," the Indian said. "The less noise we make, the better for us."

Suitably chastened, Sam ignored the bee and it finally flew away.

"Dang ornery bee," he muttered, and then lapsed into silence.

Now the only sounds were the soft hoof falls of the horses, the creak of saddle leather, and the murmur of insects among the summer wildflowers. The Kiowa leaned from the saddle and studied the trail constantly, his dark face masked in concentration.

Sam's worst fears were realized when James drew rein and pointed to the east. "They go that way."

The riders' tracks followed the arc of Reading Canyon, then headed into Goose Lake Ridge and the high timber country. There was a well-marked trail to the top of the ridge, and Sam and the Kiowa followed at a distance, riding at a slow walk to avoid raising dust.

Not far up the steep trail, James led the way onto an open, flat ledge of rock and grass about five acres in extent. Here piñon shielded the ledge from the trail and grew most of the way to a high cliff wall. From somewhere beyond the trees, Sam heard the soft splash of falling water.

"Why we stopping here?" Sam asked as the Kiowa drew rein.

"From here I go on alone, on foot," James said. "This good hideout for you, Sammy."

Sam opened his mouth to object, but the Indian got there before him.

"Up there, ridge ends, then slopes downward to upper reach of Gila," he said. "Injun-eater's place is on the west bank of river." He made a wriggling motion with his hand. "I sneak close, see what's happening." He smiled. "Then come back before nightfall and we make a good plan."

Sam, who couldn't see a red barn in front of

him, accepted the logic of that. "All right," he said, "but you take care. No brave Injun stuff."

"This Injun not so brave," James said. "Me as scared of Injun-eater Dan Wells as any Apache." The Kiowa waved a hand around the ledge. "Sammy, you find wood, make fire. Not white man's fire, small, like Indian fire. Boil coffee, fry pork, and I'll be back by nightfall."

After checking the action of his Sharps, James stepped from his horse and tossed the reins to Sam. "I go now," he said. "And see what I see."

"Good luck, James," Sam said.

The Kiowa nodded. "Don't forget coffee, huh?"

"It'll be on the bile when you get back," Sam said.

He watched James take the trail again, walking up the rise with an effortless grace, his rifle at the port.

"Maybe there's more Kiowa in you than I figgered," Sam said.

But James was already gone from sight and didn't hear him.

Chapter 12

Sam Sawyer stripped the saddles and bridles from the horses, then loosed the animals on the ledge's grass patches. There was graze enough, and water from a hidden spring at the base of the rock wall.

He gathered a supply of dry sticks that wouldn't smoke, but didn't light a fire. He'd wait until sundown arrived to herald the Kiowa's return. In the meantime he hoped that he wouldn't tangle with Apaches or a grizzly.

Sam fetched his back against a tree trunk and smoked a cigarette. The day was hot, filled with the drowsy music of bees, and the splash of water provided a soothing counterpoint. The horses munched grass, moving as little as possible, but a shod hoof now and then clinked on rock.

Sam closed his eyes and settled to a more comfortable position as he felt the ache ease in his McClellan-tormented butt. The day murmured on, the breeze a warm and pleasant breath fanning Sam's face. Sounds retreated from him, grew dim, and he slept. . . .

An hour passed. A deer clicked its way to the water, wary of the sleeping man, but driven by thirst. The animal drank and then tiptoed away on ballerina feet.

Sam slept on.

Thirty minutes after the deer left, the sound of galloping hooves shook him to wakefulness. He rose to his feet, slightly groggy, and hitched his gun into place.

Both horses had their heads up, ears pricked, looking toward the trail.

Sam drew his Colt and waited.

A few moments . . . then a horseman pounded past, heading for the top of the ridge. Man and horse were in view for a couple of seconds, and then they were gone.

A cloud of dust swirled in the rider's wake, then slowly thinned out and settled on the trail again. Sam cursed his poor vision, but blessed the piñon and juniper that had hidden him from the man's sight.

He rubbed his eyes, as though trying to dispel a vision that still lingered on his retinas. He was sure—not certain—but almost sure that the rider had been Sheriff Vic Moseley.

Sam lit a cigarette and stood hipshot, pondering this mystery.

"All right, Sam," he said aloud. "Think this thing through."

It could've been Moseley, a big man riding a sorrel hoss.

"But you're as blind as a snubbin' post," he said to himself.

He might be here to rescue Hannah and Lori.

"Or the rider might have been one of the Wells brothers, maybe ol' Starvin' Dan hisself."

Sam dropped the butt of his cigarette on the ground and rubbed it out under his heel.

This was getting him nowhere.

He'd seen a rider who looked—to a short-sighted man—like Vic Moseley. That's all he had.

Then a thought came to him.

Maybe the Kiowa saw the rider. James was a far-seeing man and wouldn't make a mistake. If it was Moseley, James would know it.

Sam looked at the blue sky and the soaring sun and wished for nightfall.

Chapter 13

The long day slowly shaded into evening, and Sam Sawyer lit the fire. At the stream, he filled the small, blackened coffeepot Mayor Meriwether had provided, and then threw in a handful of Arbuckle's. He settled the pot on the coals, and his ears reached into the night, listening for the approach of the Kiowa. He heard nothing but the rush of the spring and the rustle of the breeze in the trees.

The night birds were already pecking at the

first stars as Sam searched through a burlap sack to find out what else His Honor had so thoughtfully provided. A loaf of sourdough bread, already spotted all over with green, a slab of salt pork that didn't smell right, a small package of sugar, a twist of salt, and a slab of apple pie that didn't smell right either.

Mayor Meriwether wanted his bratty kid's skewbald pony back, but it seemed he wanted to do it as cheaply as possible.

Sam shook his head. He'd always said that men and barbed wire had their good points, but it was tough to find any in Meriwether, the mayor of Lost Mine.

Nights in the high desert country of the Gila are chilly, and Sam shivered and edged closer to his hatful of fire, his eyes probing the mysterious shadows, his mind on dead Apaches, joyless ha'nts, and the like.

Where the hell was the Kiowa? He wasn't much of an Injun to begin with. Had he ended up getting lost or captured or shot?

Sam, growing as cantankerous as all get out, growled at the night and the chill breeze and made up his mind.

He needed coffee now. "To hell with the Kiowa," he said aloud.

A distant owl asked, *Whooo?* and Sam said, "You heard me, the Kiowa."

The bird repeated the question, but this time

Sam ignored it and poured coffee into a rusted, battered tin cup with a loose handle.

He smoked a cigarette, drained his cup, poured more, and smoked another cigarette as the waxing moon rose higher in the sky and illuminated the ledge with opalescent light.

Sam threw more sticks on his lonely fire, then sought his ragged blankets that smelled of Sheriff Moseley's jail.

It took him a while, worrying and wondering about the Kiowa, but finally he slept.

The sound of a horse grazing nearby woke Sam up to morning light. He rose to his feet, shifted his holstered Colt into place, and spent the next couple of minutes working the kinks out of his back and hips. Volcanic rock a comfortable bed does not make, he decided.

Sam restarted the fire, boiled up coffee, then breakfasted on a thick sandwich of toasted bread and broiled salt pork. As he chewed, he contemplated his next move.

First things first: He'd need to scout around for James. After that, he'd get as close as he dared and study the lay of Dan Wells's dugout, and by that he meant the saloon, store, crib, and horse corrals.

Were Hannah and Lori held prisoner there? That was something else he'd need to find out.

Sam sighed deep in his chest. It was a lot to ask

of a man with nearsighted eyes and no skill as a gun hand.

And what about Vic Moseley? Was it really him he'd seen on the trail yesterday? If it was him, what was he doing in Dan Wells's territory?

Sam asked himself plenty of questions, but his answers didn't amount to a hill of beans, which wasn't surprising since he had none. After he threw the last of the coffee on the fire, Sam moved both saddles and bridles to the base of the rock wall where they'd be out of sight of prying eyes.

The horses would have to fend for themselves. Taking the trail to the Wells hideout was a job for a walking man. A rider could be seen from a far distance, and the Wells brothers surely had sharp outlaw eyes.

Sam left the ledge, cleared the piñon, and reluctantly stepped onto the trail.

His confidence level was no higher than the soles of his boots.

Chapter 14

All a worrying man does is ride a rocking horse that doesn't get him anywhere.

Sam Sawyer recognized that fact and did his best to concentrate on the job at hand. He kept off the marked trail as much as possible, making his stumbling way through thickets of juniper and brush, wary of becoming a target for a hidden marksman.

But after an hour of walking, he'd seen no one. Once a black bear stopped to study him, then huffed its disdain and strolled away, as though the doings of a scrawny old cowboy weren't worthy of its notice.

The trail peaked, then abruptly sloped downward. The high pinnacles of the Mogollon Mountains were now in sight, silhouetted against the bright sky, but all Sam saw was a blur. He knew they were mountains all right, but the size, shape, and distance of them, he couldn't tell.

Downhill walking was easier, and Sam made faster progress, though he constantly got his feet tangled in brush and roots and he fell twice, whispering cusses when what he wanted was to bellow.

Thirty minutes before the noon hour by Sam's watch, he found the Kiowa.

"Ankle's busted," the Indian said. Then, to make matters worse, he added, "I mean, real bad." James lay on his back in brush, his moccasined foot neatly wedged between two almost rectangular rocks. His rifle lay beside him, the stock broken.

Sam read the signs. "How the hell did you step in a hole?" he said.

"Because I didn't see it. That's how the hell I stepped in a hole."

Sam said, "You're the most useless man I ever met."

James said nothing, but he grimaced as Sam tugged on his leg.

"Nah, it's stuck fast. I'm gonna have to move the rocks," Sam said, irritated to the point of anger.

The Kiowa became defensive. "It wasn't my fault. Ankle busted and rifle busted." He glared at Sam. "I go home now."

"The hell you will," Sam said. "You're my eyes. I need you right here."

"I can't walk. I go home."

"You'll walk. I'll fix you up with a crutch, do you just fine." Sam stared down the Kiowa, then said, "What about your wife an' young'un? If you give up and don't come back with the skewbald pony, Moscley will kill them, and you, or worse."

"Maybe he don't care no more," James said.

"He cares about something, I reckon. I think I saw him yesterday, headed for the Wells place."

That got the Kiowa's attention. "Are you sure of that, Sammy?"

"No, I ain't sure. But I reckon it was him I seen on the trail. Hell, it had to be him."

"Why would Moseley be here?"

"If the yellow-haired woman you saw was Hannah Stewart, he could be trying to save her."

"Then it's a good time for me to leave. Moseley won't be in Lost Mine. I can get my family and light a shuck. Go far away."

"And leave me here without eyes?"

"Come with me, Sammy. You don't give a hill of beans about the skewbald pony any longer."

"You're right about that, I don't. But I do care about Hannah and her daughter."

"And I care about my own wife and daughter," the Kiowa said.

Sam Sawyer was a patient man, but he had his limits. His gun skinned from the holster and he stuck the muzzle between the Indian's eyes. "Here's how it's gonna be," he said. "If it turns out that it ain't Hannah you saw, but it is Moseley I saw, we play it your way and light a shuck."

"And if I don't cotton to that plan?" James said.

"Then I'll scatter your brains. And I mean right now."

"The white man always makes good argument when he holds gun to Indian's head."

"Do we play it my way?"

"Do I have a choice?"

"I just gave you a choice. You stick, or I blow your damned brains out."

"Then we do it your way. But only until you know if the Hannah woman is with the Indian-eater."

Sam holstered his Colt. "You're a wiser man than I thought," he said.

James's ankle was not as badly injured as Sam had originally feared, but it was hugely swollen and the Kiowa couldn't put any weight on it.

"I don't think it's broke," Sam said. "Sprained, but not broke."

"It ain't *your* ankle," James said. "It hurts real bad and I say it's broke."

Sam took off his hat and scratched his head, trying to puzzle his way through this setback. Finally he said, "Well, broke or no broke, we still got it to do."

It took Sam an hour to find a suitable Y-shaped tree branch. But even after he cut it free and trimmed it up, it was still a gnarled, crooked chunk of wood.

"It ain't much of a crutch," the Kiowa said, eying the thing.

"Well, it's the best I can do," Sam said. "Up on your feet and give it a try."

Sam watched as James settled the crutch in his armpit and attempted a few hobbling steps.

"Crackerjack!" he said. "You'll be running around in no time at all."

The Kiowa tripped and fell flat on his face.

"It'll take a bit of getting used to, is all," Sam said.

After just five minutes and three more tumbles by the Kiowa, Sam Sawyer was forced to admit that the crutch wasn't working.

And worse, if someone came up the trail, James would never be able to get out of the way and hide in the brush in time.

His face dry with grief, Sam said, "James, split ass back down the trail to the rock ledge. You'll find grub and the makings for coffee."

"What will you do, Sammy?" the Kiowa said. "Declare your intentions."

"My intention is to get close enough to see what's goin' on, I reckon," Sam said.

"I'm sorry about the rifle," James said. "It would have helped."

"Don't make no difference. I was never much of a hand with a long gun anyhow."

Sam pulled the Kiowa to his feet.

"I don't know the why of it, but I've got a nagging feeling that Moseley might be in cahoots with Dan Wells about something and is still with him. So you got time to climb on your hoss and save your wife and kid," he said.

"But you have no eyes."

"Then I guess I'll have to make do with the pair of throwaways the good Lord seen fit to give me," Sam said.

"Be careful, Sammy."

Sam smiled. "James, a toothless dog always chews careful."

He turned the Kiowa until he was facing in the direction of their back trail.

"Now git goin'," Sam said, giving him a gentle push.

The Indian nodded. "Good luck, Sam."

He watched the Kiowa wave again, then make his painful way back to the camp.

Suddenly Sam felt very alone . . . the worst high lonesome he'd ever known in his life.

Chapter 15

"Take a good look, Hannah. Is this what you want?"

The three slatternly women lying on stained mattresses on the floor of the adobe stared at Hannah Stewart with expressions that went from sympathy to disdain to outright hostility.

"Sure, honey, come join us," said the hostile woman, a hard-eyed blonde with a knife scar below her collarbone. "At two dollars a bang, you'll be riding in a carriage in no time."

The other women laughed at the joke as Hannah said, "Why did you bring me here, Vic?"

"Because this is where you'll end up if you don't become my woman," Moseley said. "I already talked to Dan Wells and he says it's fine by him. He reckons you're a handsome woman and would be a good little earner, but he's willing to let you go."

"I'll die before I'd become your . . . anything," Hannah said.

"That can be arranged too," Moseley said. His smile was cruel.

"My daughter," Hannah said. "What about her? You used to say Lori was the joy of your life."

"That's because I was lying," Moseley said. "I don't want the brat. I sure as hell ain't raising some other man's get."

"I won't give up my child for anyone." Hannah raised a defiant face to Moseley. "You're evil, Vic Moseley. More evil than I thought a man could be."

"When I want lip from you, I'll ask for it," he said, his face black with rage.

Hannah was terrified, but her eyes were challenging. "Strike me, Vic, and I swear I'll one day kill you," she said.

Moseley drew back his hand, but he hesitated and let it drop to his side. "I'll break you, Hannah," he said. "Dan Wells is an expert and he'll show me how."

"A low-life scum like you won't break me," Hannah said. "Now take me to my daughter."

"Lori is safe . . . for now," Moseley said. "Maybe I'll let you see her later." He grabbed

Hannah's arm. "Don't count on Mayor Meriwether. He don't give a damn about you. All he wants is his brat's pony back and he even hired two idiots to get it. Of course, that's all to the good. While he's fretting and worrying about a skewbald pony, I can get on with my business."

"And what is your business here?" Hannah said. "Me?"

"You flatter yourself, lady. Well, yeah, sure, you're part of it, but me and Dan Wells have another, more important iron in the fire."

Moseley's smirk was mocking. "After I tire of you, I'll kick you out and you can go look for your daughter. Me, I'd try Old Mexico first."

Hannah flushed with anger. "You bastard!" she said. She tried to slap Moseley across the face, but he caught her wrist and dragged her out the door.

Twenty yards beyond the adobe, a small dugout with a heavy timber door had been carved out of the mountain slope.

Moseley drew back the bolt and threw Hannah into the dark interior.

"You can cool off in here," he said. "And when I come back for you, I'd advise you to be a sight more accommodating."

The sheriff shut the door and slammed the bolt home.

Hannah was left in darkness with her anger and her fear.

• • •

"How you getting along with the Stewart woman?" Dan Wells said.

"She'll come round," Moseley said. "Enough about women. We have more important things to discuss, so let's get down to business. I don't have much time."

"Meriwether keeps you on a short leash, huh, Vic?"

"I don't want to arouse his suspicions, that's all." He stared into Wells's black eyes. "Nobody keeps Vic Moseley on a leash."

Wells raised his hands. "No offense intended, I'm sure."

"Should Jake and Jeptha be in on this?" Moseley said.

Wells shook a shaved head as big, round, and hard as a cannonball. "They're out hunting for the two men Meriwether hired to bring back the skewbald pony. I don't want a broken-down puncher and a blanket Indian poking their noses into my affairs."

"I'll take the pony back myself, get in good with Meriwether," Moseley said. "Can we depend on your brothers to take care of the puncher?"

"Jake and Jeptha don't have the brains of a grasshopper, but they'll find and gun them two men, depend on it."

Moseley nodded. Then he smiled. "Funny

thing, Dan, the reason Meriwether hired those men is that he thinks I'm afraid of you."

For a while Wells just sat and stared at the sheriff and said nothing.

Then, finally, "If you ain't, Vic, you should be."

Moseley heard the words and felt a shiver run down his spine, as if snow had just fallen on his grave.

Chapter 16

Sam Sawyer could see well enough to recognize the Gila River twisting like a serpent through the valley floor below him. Beyond the river rose the skyward, timber-covered peaks of the Mogollons.

He was sure it was the Wells place that lay on the slope below him, a flat ledge of rock that weather and time had carved out of the mountainside.

He screwed up his eyes, straining to see more.

A corral beside a dugout—maybe. A small adobe building—maybe. A hog rooting around at the rim of the ledge where it overhung the river—maybe.

To his chagrin, he knew he could be looking only at a sheer rock face and a grazing elk.

If a sharp eye is the mother of good luck, right then Sam figured he was an orphan.

Beside him a cricket played fiddle in the grass and the sun burned in a sky the color of faded denim. The day was stifling and only the river and the mountains looked cool.

Sam considered his options, then summed them up when he decided he had only one—he'd have to get closer.

A lot closer.

The downward game trail would stop at the river, the water low at this time of year, so long after the spring melt.

He'd take the path to the river and make another decision then, when the landscape came into focus.

Sam followed the trail downward until he could make out the riverbank, fringed with cottonwood, alder, willow, and a few maple and ash, the trees underpinned with brush and scattered wildflowers.

Here, under the blue sky, the Gila flowed bright and slow and trout glided elegantly along its shady moss banks.

There was a crossing nearby, only a couple of feet deep, marked with river rocks. Sam ignored that and walked west for a hundred yards, keeping to the trees, away from prying eyes.

He stood in the shelter of a cottonwood and, closer now, studied the sunbaked rock ledge. The place was more in focus, but to Sam it looked as though he saw it through water.

There really was an adobe building. He'd been right about that. And he thought he could make out the rough timber doors to a couple of dugouts. The hog was really a hog and still rooted on the rim, but beyond that he could make out little.

Of the skewbald pony there was no sign. Nor was there any trace of a woman and child who could be Hannah and Lori.

Sam squatted and rocked back on his heels. He could hole up here in the cover of the trees until nightfall, then scout for Hannah and the pony.

It seemed like a plan, but Sam was gloomy. Prowling around in the dark wasn't a job for a man with bad eyes and the rheumatisms.

He settled down to wait, wishful for a smoke, but not daring to light a cigarette.

"What the hell are you?"

The voice came from Sam's left and he turned his head slowly.

The man watching him was the size of a grizzly, his huge, shaggy head supported by a bull neck, roped with muscle. The big man's eyes were mildly amused, but, shortsighted as he was, Sam saw cruelty in the man's stare and an unheeding brutality in every massive inch of him. He led a beautiful sorrel horse with a silver-mounted Mexican saddle and bridle.

"Howdy," Sam said, smiling. He stood. "And

I'm right pleased to meet you, seeing as how I'm just passin' through an' all."

The man was dressed in greasy buckskins, his guns carried butts forward in a thick black belt with a silver CSA buckle.

"What the hell are you doing here, skulking in the trees?" the man said. His voice sounded like a rusty gate hinge badly in need of oil.

"Well," Sam said, trying his best to sound like a pilgrim, "I was headed for Silver City where I hope to prosper in the restaurant business, but I reckon I must've taken a wrong turn. I decided to rest here for a spell."

"Silver City is due south," the man said. "You're headed due east."

"Ah," Sam said, "so that's where I made my mistake."

"I got a feeling you're making another," the giant said. "Where's your hoss?"

Sam blinked and said, "Yesterday mornin' he got spooked by a rattlesnake and bolted on me and I ain't seen him since."

The man nodded, as though agreeing that horses and rattlesnakes never could get along. But then he said, "You're a liar."

Now, Sam recognized that as fighting talk, but he was in no position to take offense. The man was a big target, but he was nowhere close enough for accurate shooting—at least on Sam's part.

"Sorry to hear you say that, mister," Sam said. "I take it that you ain't exactly an amiable man."

"Your name is Sam Sawyer, a bust-up puncher out of Texas and low-down. You came here to steal the skewbald pony my brother took in Lost Mine a few days back."

Seeing the surprised look on Sam's face, the man said, "Vic Moseley told us all about you." He glanced around him. "Where's the Indian?"

"Ankle got busted," Sam said, knowing he could be counting the rest of his life in seconds. "He headed home, hurting real bad."

"You lyin' to me?"

"No, I ain't. It's the honest truth." Sam made a sign on his chest. "Cross my heart and hope to die."

"What am I gonna do with you?" the man asked.

"Let me go? Then I'll bid you good day and continue on my way."

"No, that ain't gonna happen." The big man smiled. There was no humor in the grimace, just cruelty. "I could take you back to brother Dan." He snorted and chopped his yellow teeth together. "He could eat you like he et the Comanch'."

The man dropped the reins of his horse and pulled a bowie from the sheath on his belt. "Or I can see how you look skun. Be fun to watch your guts fall out."

The writing was on the wall, and Sam prayed that the man would come closer. He needed to be within spitting distance.

Taking a chance, he said, "You ain't gonna skin nobody, you piece of trash."

Draw him close. Draw him close.

The man took a single step toward Sam, grinning, his thumb testing the edge of his blade.

"My name's Jeptha Wells," he said. "That name is famous all over the territory. Now you know me, don't it make you sceered?"

"Never heard of you," Sam said. "I don't pay much mind when folks talk about riffraff and tinhorns."

Sam's strategy worked.

Stung, Jeptha Wells bellowed in rage and ran toward the older man, his knife low and ready.

Luckily for Sam, Wells's heart was set on a skinning, not revolver work. Sam dived to his right. His shoulder slammed into the ground. It didn't hurt right then, but he knew it would later.

As he fell, he pulled his Colt and thumbed back the hammer. His right shoulder was numb, but he was able to push his gun straight out in front of him.

He pulled the trigger.

Against all the odds, his aim was true.

Hit high in the chest, Wells staggered back a step, his face ashen from shock. He knew right then that he'd taken a killing shot, and now it transformed him into a dangerous, wounded animal.

A terrible roar of rage, and then the big man made a header for Sam, the bowie up for a plunging death stroke.

Sam had a split second to think about it—fire again or get the hell out of the way. He chose the latter.

Fear made him spry. A moment before Wells would have landed on him, he rolled quickly to his right. But he'd forgotten how close he was to the river. He tumbled over the bank and hit the water, scattering fish.

Wells was on his feet in an instant. He staggered to the bank, grasping his bowie above his head, intent on diving on top of Sam again.

Water running into his eyes, Sam fired. Fired again. Missed with both shots.

He waded away from the bank and glanced fearfully over his shoulder.

Wells didn't dive into the water. He jumped in with both feet and this time he had a gun in his hand.

Sam fired into the splash, but he thought he'd done no execution.

Wells was on his feet, legs spread against the current, his Colt up at waist level. He fired.

Sam felt the shock of the bullet, like a blow from a fence post swung by a strong man, to his lower left ribs.

He staggered, almost fell on a slippery rock, but recovered his balance.

"You done for me, but I've got ye now," Wells said. "Damn you, you can cook me supper in hell."

Sam had one round left in the cylinder. He two-handed his Colt to eye level and squeezed the trigger.

At first he thought he'd missed again, because Wells stood his ground. The big man shot twice, three times, all his bullets flying wild.

But Sam's last round had hit home.

His chest running scarlet with blood from two wounds, Wells finally dropped to his knees and pitched forward into the river, fountains of water erupting around him.

Blood stained the river, spreading out from the big man like rust, and Sam stepped aside as the huge spread-eagled body slowly floated past.

For a few moments Sam watched Jeptha Wells bob facedown in the river and then he shook his head. "Mister," he said, "never trust a wolf until it's been skun."

Dripping wet, he waded for the bank, then stopped to holster his gun.

A bullet kicked up a startled exclamation point of water less than a foot from where he stood.

Two men were shooting at him. One stood on a hard talus incline that sloped down from the rock ledge. The other was already on the riverbank, a rifle to his shoulder.

Wading as fast as he could, Sam again made for the bank, bullets ripping up the air around him.

He clambered onto dry ground and saw to his joy that Wells's horse was still there. The sorrel was an outlaw's mount and had been trained to stand.

Sam stepped into the saddle, swung the horse around, away from the gunmen, and kicked the animal into a gallop.

Probing bullets followed him, rattling through tree branches, and he heard angry shouts as someone found Jeptha Wells's body.

The game trail along the riverbank made a swing to the west and followed the course of the Gila.

A long canyon wind and the hot sun began to dry Sam's wet duds. He put a hand to his ribs and it came away covered in blood and he knew a moment of panic.

How badly was he hurt?

The only way to answer that question was to find a safe place to hole up and see if he was carrying Wells's lead.

Sam heard no sound of pursuit and felt secure enough to ride into the shelter of the trees, the tobacco hunger on him.

By some miracle his makings were still dry, but after he built a cigarette he used up all his damp matches. His last and final hope barely flared into fire, but the flame lasted long enough to light his smoke.

Sam looked around him, dragging deep on his cigarette, the pain in his ribs gnawing at him.

"Sam," he said aloud through a sigh, "no matter how you sum it up, you're in one helluva fix."

He was fresh out of ideas and no closer to rescuing Hannah and Lori. Worse, he might be shot through and through, maybe even dying.

And worse still, he'd killed Jeptha Wells and now brother Dan would soon be on his trail, hunting revenge.

Sam sighed deep and long. "What a fix I'm in," he said again.

He glanced down at the blood on his shirt and figured he was bleeding hard. It had to be a serious wound—as if there was any other kind.

The sorrel was up on its toes, ready for the trail, and Sam kneed the big horse into motion.

He felt like a man climbing the gallows steps to his own hanging.

Chapter 17

Vic Moseley grinned when he heard the shot. "I guess your brothers caught up with them two idiots," he said.

"Seems like," Dan Wells said. "Jeptha and Jake have done for them."

"It's no great loss," Moseley said, grinning.

But when more shots echoed through the river canyon, Wells jumped to his feet and grabbed his Winchester.

"Hell," he said, "that isn't a shooting. It's a blasted gunfight."

Moseley didn't get up. "Relax, Dan," he said. "It's only the boys having some fun. We got important business to discuss."

"Later," Wells said as another shot blasted. "That came from the river. I'm gonna take a look-see."

Moseley's eyes followed Wells out the door.

He hesitated a moment, and then he too got to his feet. Anger pinching at him, he went after Wells.

Thirty thousand in cash money was a lot more important to him than the well-being of Dan Wells's crazy brothers.

As Moseley started on the slope from the ledge to the bank, he stopped when he saw Dan Wells shooting at a man in the river.

The sheriff watched Sam Sawyer clamber up the far bank, and took a pot at him. He missed and then watched as Sam stepped into the saddle of Jeptha's horse.

Wells stood on the bank, a Winchester to his shoulder. He fired and Moseley saw Sam reel in the saddle.

"Dan, you got the son of a gun!" Moseley yelled.

The three women stood at the rim of the edge, enjoying the show. A skinny man wearing a white apron, a scattergun in his hands, joined them.

Moseley wore hand-sewn, hundred-dollar boots, and he wasn't about to get them wet fishing a body out of the river. He contented himself by taking another hopeless pot at the fleeing Sam.

Dan Wells was almost at midstream before he grabbed his brother's body. Jeptha had snagged on a submerged tree branch and his huge carcass rocked gently in the current. Wells dragged the body to the bank and Moseley helped him haul it onto dry land.

After he turned Jeptha on his back, Wells gazed down at the lifeless face. His brother's eyes were wide open, staring into some terrifying eternity. His wounds still seeped blood.

"I'm sorry about this, Dan," Moseley said. "Real sorry."

Wells said nothing.

Then he tipped his head back and emitted a high-pitched, dreadful scream, the frightened-woman shriek of the hunting cougar.

Moseley felt his spine ice, and was surprised that his hands trembled.

Wells turned to him, his eyes on fire.

"Who," he said, his voice hollow, like a whisper from a tomb, "was it?"

"His name is Sam," Moseley said.

"That's all? Just Sam?"

"I don't remember his last name." Then, to make up for his forgetfulness: "He's a broken-down puncher who hopes to prosper in the restaurant trade."

"He will not prosper," Wells said. The skin of his face was tight, giving it the look of a yellow skull. "His death will be long and painful."

Up until then, Moseley had been afraid of no man. But the realization came to him that he feared Dan Wells.

"Dan," he said, "we need to talk about the army payroll. Time is money."

"There will be no talk of money until my brother is avenged," Wells said.

He stared at Moseley. "We'll find Jake and bring him in. He must attend his brother's burying." Wells rose to his feet. "Wait. You know this man, this Sam. After Jeptha is laid to rest, you will ride with me and point him out. I'll kill him wherever he may be."

Moseley felt a fortune slipping through his fingers. But when he looked at Dan Wells, he saw only death. This was not the time or the place to mention gold again.

"I'll ride with you," he said, the words dropping from his lips like lead weights.

• • •

Jake Wells favored Jeptha more than he did his brother Dan.

Where Dan Wells was a blade of steel, tempered to tough slenderness, Jake was huge, with a shaggy mane of red hair and a beard that spread over his buckskinned chest to the buckle of his gun belt.

He was twice as big as Dan, but only half as smart.

During his career as an outlaw, Dan Wells had killed three white men, Jake seven—only one of them in a fair fight.

As he watched the last shovelful of dirt thrown on Jeptha's grave, Jake played "In the Sweet By and By" on his harmonica.

Dan Wells, much affected, threw back his head and, his eyes streaming tears, joined the harmonica in song.

In the sweet by and by,
We shall meet on that beautiful shore;
In the sweet by and by,
We shall meet on that beautiful shore.

The harmonica wailed to an end and Jake threw himself on the grave, sobbing. He was crazed with grief and filled with the hunger to strike out and maim and kill.

At that moment he was the most dangerous man on earth.

Chapter 18

Sam Sawyer followed the river trail west along the bank of the Gila, then looped to the south as the massive bulk of Watson Mountain blocked his path.

He had lost blood and felt as weak as a day-old kitten, and the pain of his wounded ribs gave him no peace. Sweat beaded his forehead, and shimmering heat waves banked around him, adding to his misery.

Under a pitiless sun, riding through the thin air, Sam looped west again into the Canyon Hills at the foot of the Pinos Altos Range. He desperately needed a place to hole up and treat his wound.

Sam drew rein and looked around him. He saw little but mountain peaks and the green swath of high timber under the hazy bowl of the sky.

Born of the Mogollon Mountains to the northwest, a sudden wind took Sam by surprise. Around him mesquite and juniper clicked their branches, and higher on the Pinos Altos slopes aspen trembled, to the amused rustle of the swaying pines.

The wind grew in intensity, and Sam felt the sting of desert sand on his face. Shredded leaves and pine needles cartwheeled around him, and the sorrel grew restive and tossed its head, jangling the bit.

The horse had begun its career as a cow pony, and from the dim shadows of its memory came the recollection that this was stampede weather, and dangerous.

Roaring now, the wind pummeled Sam as he swung out of the saddle and led the sorrel toward what he hoped was the mouth of a narrow arroyo. He had no confidence in his sight, and he might well be heading straight for a U-shaped slab of dark rock.

A loud *crack!* cut through the deeper bellow of the storm as the wind snapped a ponderosa pine. The tree toppled over and bled sap from a splintered stump.

Spooked, the sorrel reared, frightened arcs of white in its eyes.

"Easy, boy, easy," Sam said, holding on to the reins for grim life.

But weakened as he was by loss of blood, the reins wrenched out of his hands as the big sorrel reared again, this time twisting its head away.

The horse turned, felt the wind under its tail, and bolted. It skirted the foothills, and Sam quickly lost sight of the animal as it galloped south.

Cussing under his breath, he made for what he believed was the arroyo.

To his unbounded joy, it was.

• • •

The rocky gully was narrow, not much wider than a slot canyon, and it was choked with brush and cactus. Sam had trouble making his way deeper as he searched for a place out of the wind where he could sit and rest.

Mesquite and juniper grew on top of sheer rock walls that were about ten feet high. Above Sam's head the trees rustled and creaked, hammered by gusts that shrieked like banshees.

After about twenty yards, the arroyo opened up into a small amphitheater enclosed by tall spikes of raw white rock. Here there was grass, but no sign of water.

Sam found a spot in the lee of the wind, sat down, and gratefully fetched his back against the warm rock. He reached for the makings, remembered that he had no matches, and felt the bitter disappointment that only a smoking man knows.

Steeling himself for the worst, he slipped his canvas suspenders off his shoulders and opened his shirt. Shifting his body around, he craned his head to inspect his wound.

It didn't look good. In fact, it seemed real bad.

His entire left side was thick with dried blood, and when he touched his ribs the pain took his breath away and made him wince.

"Blast it, Sam," he said. "I reckon you're shot through and through like you thought."

He had no water to bathe the wound and figured it wouldn't help anyway. Maybe he was done for. Maybe he was breathing his last, and him without a smoke.

Sadder still, his shirt was ruined, and he bitterly regretted the forty-five cents he'd paid for it in El Paso just a couple of years before.

It had been a real nice shirt.

A ravening wind is the wild, bastard child of a high-country thunderstorm, and Sam heard distant rumbles as the sky turned to molten lead.

There was no shelter in the clearing and he knew to steer clear of the few stunted trees that grew here and there. Up in the Spur Lake country he'd once seen a horse and rider killed by lightning after they took shelter under a wild oak, and the memory lived with him.

Sam drew up his knees and bent his head, waiting for what was to come. Good or bad, he no longer cared.

Lightning scrawled across the sky like the signature of a demented pagan god.

Then came thunder.

Then came the rain.

The downpour battered Sam's shoulders and rattled on his hat like a kettledrum. The clearing seared white in the lightning flashes, and the rain-running rock shimmered like wet steel. Thunder slammed into the arroyo, echoing like a cannonade, and he heard another pine groan, then break.

Sam wrapped his arms around his chest, trying to make himself small, miserable in his loneliness.

Hunched against the storm as Sam was, the rider took him by surprise.

Chapter 19

A boom of thunder that rattled the door of the dugout wakened Hannah Stewart from uneasy sleep.

Rain hissed around her like a baby dragon under a rock, and lightning flared though the inch-wide gap between the door and jamb.

She rose from a pile of sacking, stepped to the door, pressed her face to a gap, and looked outside. As far as she could tell, her view confined to a narrow slit, the only thing moving out there was the rain.

There was no sign of Vic Moseley or the Wells brothers.

Earlier—had it been an hour ago or a day?—she'd heard shooting, and much later the sound of horses moving out. Did that mean Moseley and the others were gone, at least for a while?

Hannah had no answer to that question, but it didn't really matter. Lori was still held captive, either in the saloon or the women's quarters, and she had to find her.

The heavy door presented a problem, since she didn't have the strength to force it open.

Waiting for lightning flashes to illuminate her way, she searched around the dugout. She found nothing but a rusty steel eating fork and some coiled rope.

The fork she could use.

The outside bolt was a heavy piece of timber that slotted into a U-shaped iron bracket. About an inch of the bolt showed between the ill-fitting door and the jamb.

Hannah slipped the head of the fork into the space. She jabbed the prongs into the timber and tried to use them to ease back the bolt.

It didn't work. The tines were too blunt and fragile to penetrate the tough pine.

She tried again, with the same result—the bolt refused to budge.

Frowning, Hannah thumbed the prongs. Then she stepped to the rear wall of the dugout. Her face set in concentration, she began to scrape the steel handle of the fork against the rock.

After an hour of steady work, Hannah stepped to the door again and looked outside. The storm still raged. The rain that lashed in torrents across the ledge in front of the dugouts had already turned the dirt to mud. Here and there amid the downpour, puddles had formed, erupting all over in jolting Vs of water.

No one would dare venture outside, and Hannah returned to her task.

It took another hour of steady work before she managed to hone a passable point on the fork handle.

She held the fork up to watery light slanting through the door and studied its sharpness. Hannah made a face. It wasn't great, but it would have to do.

Stepping to the door again, she rammed the sharpened fork into the timber with all the strength she could muster. This time the point sank about an eighth of an inch into the wood, and Hannah felt a little thrill of triumph.

She pushed on the fork and then tried to start the bolt sliding back. It moved just a fraction. But it was a start.

Another try and it moved again.

A full hour passed before Hannah worked the bolt back enough that it slid out of the iron bracket and the door swung open on creaking hinges. Her fingers ached and the tines of the fork had dug into her right palm, raising painful welts. But now she was free to find her child and leave this terrible place.

Hannah slipped the fork into the pocket of her dress as a weapon, hiked up her skirts, and ran into the raking rain.

The door to the adobe was closed against the weather, but Hannah didn't hesitate. Strands of wet hair falling over her face, she slammed the door open and rushed inside, the sharpened fork in her right hand.

The three women were startled. They'd been sitting on a cot, apparently deep in conversation, and now they jumped to their feet.

Hannah waved her makeshift weapon. "Where is my daughter?" she said. "Where is Lori?"

Lorelei was the first to recover from Hannah's dramatic entrance. "Put the sticker down, schoolma'am, and we'll talk," she said.

Hannah looked around her. "For Pete's sake, where is she?"

"The kid's safe," Lorelei said.

"Where is she?"

"In the saloon, with Matt Laurie, the bartender," Lorelei said. "Moseley told him to keep an eye on her."

Hannah immediately turned to leave, but the other woman's voice stopped her.

"Wait!" she said. "Laurie is as mean as a snake and he's got himself an L. C. Smith scattergun that's both wife and child to him. He'll kill a woman just as fast as he will a man."

"He's done it before," said another woman, a small blonde with dark shadows under her eyes. She said to Lorelei, "Remember Mary Sullivan?"

Lorelei didn't answer, her eyes reading Hannah's face. "No matter what, you're going into the saloon to get your daughter back, ain't you?"

"Yes," Hannah said, an angry mama cougar in search of her cub. "And I'm doing it right now."

"Then I'm coming with you," Lorelei said.

"Please, you don't have to risk—"

"I'm coming with you," Lorelei said. "For once in my life, let me try and do something decent."

"Lorelei, if you cross him, Matt Laurie will kill you fer sure," the blonde said, alarmed. "You know how he is. He's crazy."

Lorelei took a Remington derringer from the drawstring purse she kept under her bed.

"He'll kill me if I don't kill him first," she said. "And yes, I remember Mary Sullivan. How could I forget her? She was my sister."

Chapter 20

The two women stepped out of the adobe into teeming rain. The thunderstorm lingered. Lightning slashed across the iron gray sky, and thunder growled and roared like a bee-stung bear.

Their high-button boots splashing through water and mud, Hannah and Lorelei ran for the saloon.

Lorelei stopped at the door and said, "Are you ready?"

Hannah didn't trust her voice not to shake and she settled for a quick nod.

"No matter what I say, you go along with it, understand?" Lorelei said.

She looked for a reply in Hannah's pale face, and repeated, "Do you understand?"

Hannah nodded, and Lorelei said, "Then let's do it, schoolma'am."

Lorelei opened the door and Hannah followed her inside.

Matt Laurie was quick and he wasn't a trusting man. He reached behind the bar and laid his shotgun on the counter.

"What the hell are you doing here, Lorelei?" he said. His eyes moved to Hannah. "Who let you out?"

"I did," Lorelei said. She smiled, moving a wisp of damp hair off her forehead. "We both felt the need for company, Matt."

Laurie was suspicious. It was obvious by the stiff way he held himself and the closeness of his hand to the shotgun. But a woman can cloud a man's thinking.

"What kind of company do you have in mind, Lorelei?" he said. He brushed his mustache with his forefinger, and his black eyes glittered.

"Where's my daughter?" Hannah demanded.

The bartender jerked a thumb over his shoulder.

"Back there in the storeroom. Nothing to harm her but whiskey barrels and maybe rats."

"I'm going to her," Hannah said. She crossed the floor, her heels thudding on the saloon's stone floor.

Laurie's shotgun came up. "Sheriff Moseley says nobody sees the brat until he gets back, so stay right where you're at. I got all kinds of faith in this here scattergun."

Moving quickly, Lorelei crossed the floor, getting between Hannah and the shotgun. "Don't mind the schoolma'am, Matt," she said.

"I don't want no trouble with her, Lorelei," Laurie said. "I don't want no trouble with Dan Wells either."

"There will be no trouble, Matt," Lorelei said. "Hannah's just upset about her kid. She'll get over it."

"Sheriff Moseley says she can see the kid when he gets back," the bartender said. "That's what he told me, and I do as he says."

Lorelei glared at Hannah, her eyes telegraphing her concern.

"Well, that's just fine, isn't it?" she said. "You can wait until Vic gets back, can't you, schoolma'am, you being his picked woman an' all?"

"Hell, Lorelei, I don't want no trouble with Vic Moseley either," Laurie said.

"Tell you what, Matt," Lorelei said. "Why don't you come over here and give me a kiss?"

Laurie's eyes went to the dugout's only glazed window, and for a few moments he watched the rain stream down the panes. "Well . . . ," he said.

"A big, strong man like you," Lorelei said, with a dove's professional sincerity.

Laurie grinned. His teeth were few in number, and those that remained were black. "Then let's get her done," he said, talking through saliva.

"Then come out from behind the counter, you big lug," Lorelei said, smiling.

Made careless by desire, Laurie left the counter . . . and walked belly-first into a .41-caliber bullet.

The man's face was stricken as he staggered back.

"Lorelei, you gut-shot me," he said, his eyes shocked, unbelieving.

"So I did," the woman said, smoke trickling from the little gun in her hand.

Lorelei's face showed no emotion, and watching her, Hannah felt a shiver. How could a woman kill that way? So coldly, as though she had no soul?

It seemed that Matt Laurie was just as dumb-struck. The hand he held to his belly seeped blood through his fingers, and his face was ashen.

"Why?" he said. "Why did you do that?"

"I always planned on killing you, Matt," Lorelei said as she loaded another bullet in her gun. "Right now seemed as good a time as any."

Bent over his wound, Laurie backed toward the bar.

"I never did nothing to you, Lorelei."

The woman smiled, humorless as a hangman.

"Remember Mary Sullivan, the little gal who loved to sing, Matt? Remember how you cut her in half with your shotgun when she tried to leave you after you beat her one time too many? You remember that?"

"She was nothing to you," Laurie said.

"She was my sister."

Laurie turned and made a staggering reach for the shotgun.

Lorelei fired again, and this time the man went down and then rolled onto his back, staring at her.

"Get your daughter," Lorelei yelled to Hannah, her face wreathed in gray gun smoke.

Hannah stepped warily around Laurie. Then she ran for the storeroom behind the bar.

After Hannah left, Lorelei got a bottle of whiskey from the bar and tossed it onto Laurie's prone body.

"You've got two bullets in your belly, Matt," she said. "And you'll be a long time a-dying. The whiskey won't make it any easier, but in your case it'll stand in place of prayers."

"Curse you, Lorelei," Laurie said through teeth

117

gritted against pain. "Put one in between my eyes. Get it over with."

The woman shook her head. "Mister, the whiskey is as far as I go. I'm doing you no more favors."

Hannah returned with Lori. The child seemed unharmed, though her eyes widened in terror and she clutched onto her mother when she saw the wounded man writhing on the floor.

Lorelei grabbed the shotgun and motioned to Hannah to leave.

"There are horses in the barn," she said. "Saddle a couple while I round up some grub."

"What about him?" Hannah said.

"What about him?"

"Shouldn't we help him?"

"He's beyond help," Lorelei said. "I gave him a bottle. That's all the help he gets."

Hannah opened her mouth to speak, but the other woman pushed her toward the door. "There's no time for talking. Get the horses saddled. We sure as hell don't want to be here when Moseley and Dan Wells get back."

When Lorelei showed up at the barn, she carried a sack of supplies and a couple of yellow slickers. She wore two battered hats on her head.

She tied the sack to her saddle horn, then handed one of the slickers to Hannah. "And this'll keep the rain off that nice yellow hair," she said, removing one of the shapeless hats. "Now let's ride."

Hannah shrugged into the slicker and settled the hat on her head.

"Now you don't look so much like a schoolma'am," Lorelei said. She smiled. "I don't know what the hell you look like."

Both women mounted and Hannah took Lori up in front of her.

"Where are we headed?" Hannah said.

"To London to have tea with the queen," Lorelei said. "How should I know where we're headed? Well away from here—that's fer sure."

"We could go to my place up near Haystack Mountain," Hannah said.

"First place Moseley would look for us, there and at Lost Mine," Lorelei said. She managed a smile. "Cheer up, schoolma'am. I'll figure something out." She kneed her horse into motion. "Silver City, maybe, where there's law."

Lorelei led the way out of the barn and into the steel curtain of the rain.

At first Hannah thought she'd heard a blast of thunder, but when she looked at Lorelei the woman was clutching her right shoulder, blood trickling through her fingers.

A second shot split the air above Hannah's head. Then she saw him.

Matt Laurie stood at the door of the saloon,

supporting himself with one hand on the frame, his other raised to eye level, working a Colt.

Lorelei swung her horse around. "Let's get the hell away from here!"

A few ineffective shots followed them as the women left the shelf and hit the ancient, hardened talus slope at a run.

Their horses' hooves kicking up scattering showers of shale and gravel, they cleared the slope and reached the flat. Hannah followed as Lorelei swung north along the Gila.

As Watson Mountain came into view, they crossed the river at a fast-running shallow and took the trail as it looped west.

Thunder crashed above the women's heads, and blue lightning branded the sky and smelled of ozone. Lori sheltered under Hannah's slicker, her thumb in her mouth, her eyes wide and scared.

"We have to find shelter soon," Hannah yelled above the bedlam of the storm.

Lorelei nodded but said nothing.

Her face was white in the lightning flashes and she turned quickly away from Hannah so the woman wouldn't see the pink blood mingled with rain that ran down the front of her yellow slicker.

Chapter 21

Sam Sawyer jumped to his feet, his hand clawing for his gun, as the rider entered the clearing at a slow walk.

Thunder roared above him as Sam barked a challenge that the rider didn't hear. In the lull that followed he yelled again, "Stay right there or I'll drill ya."

Lashed by rain, the rider lifted his head. "Sammy, you're as blind as a posthole. It's me—James."

Sam leaned forward and peered through the downpour. "Is it you?"

"Yeah, it's me, and I ain't gettin' down less'n you say you can see me, Sammy," the Kiowa said. "I ain't stupid. Now I'm getting off this pony real slow, and I don't want you cuttin' loose on me."

"You got a dry match?" Sam said, holstering his gun.

James tossed his crutch on the ground and climbed out of the saddle. His bony paint wandered away to find graze.

"How did you find me?" Sam said.

"I am Kiowa."

"I know, but you ain't exactly a prime specimen. Do you have a match?"

Rain ran off the brim of James's hat as he

moved closer to the meager shelter of the rock wall. He limped badly.

"Big wind blew me here," he said. "You leave white man's tracks. Then rain come, big storm, no more tracks."

"You got a match?" Sam said.

"I see where your horse bolted. That was clear in the grass. Then I look around and see arroyo. Only Sammy Sawyer dumb enough to hide out in a box canyon, so I come in here."

"You got a match?" Sam said.

"Maybe so," the Kiowa said.

For the first time he noticed the blood on Sam's shirt.

"You been hurt, Sammy?" he said.

"Shot through and through. I need that match."

"Let me see wound."

Sam heaved a long, silent sigh, slipped the suspender off his shoulder, and pulled up his shirt. "You ain't a doctor, James, not even a witch doctor."

"Maybe not, but when man is shot all to pieces, I usually can tell."

"You got that match handy?" Sam said. "If you have, I'd be right grateful."

The Kiowa studied Sam's wound in silence, but his head-shaking and occasional "tut-tut-tut" frayed the older man's already fiddle string nerves.

"For Pete's sake, how bad is it?" Sam yelled. "Tell me."

"A little longer," the Kiowa said, his fingers probing.

"Where's that match?" Sam said.

After another minute or so of head shaking, James wiped rain from his eyes and said, "Looks like bullet burned your ribs, Sammy. Nothing broke."

"You sure? It feels worse than that, like I'm all shot to pieces."

"Sure, I'm sure. You got burned, is all."

"I'm bleeding like a stuck hog and I hurt like the blazes."

"That's because you're a white man. If you were Indian man, no hurt at all."

"Where's that match?" Sam said.

Sam put a match to his fourth cigarette. He'd battled rain and damp makings to build his smokes, but it was worth it. The tobacco had worked its magic and his thrumming nerves had quieted.

"Why did you come back for me?" he said to the Kiowa, talking out a trail of blue smoke. He was wishful for coffee but had none.

"I was started to head home," James said, "but turned back. I heard the voices of my ancient ancestors in my head and they said that what I was doing was not the way of the warrior. They said the crazy, bad-eyed white man would be killed fer sure if I was not there to guide him. Maybe so."

"That's true-blue," Sam said. "The kind of tip-top behavior I'd expect from a white man."

"It was not true-blue," the Kiowa said. "It was stupid. The ancient ancestors are not always right."

"Well, anyhoo, I'm glad you're here," Sam said. "I needed a smoke real bad."

The Kiowa leaned a shoulder against the rock wall and asked Sam to tell him how he came by his wound.

And he did.

After Sam had finished speaking, James stood still and quiet. When he finally did speak, his voice was a broken croak.

"I told you it was stupid," he said.

The thunderstorm showed no inclination to move on, and Sam sheltered from the pounding rain as best he could while the Kiowa hobbled away to stand guard at the mouth of the arroyo.

Within ten minutes the Indian returned, his agitated face signaling his alarm.

"Riders coming, Sammy," he said. "Two men."

"Is it Moseley and Dan Wells?" Sam said.

"I don't know. I count noses and run."

"Hell, couldn't you have waited until they got closer?"

"Would you wait out there with no gun?"

Sam's nerves were twanging again and suddenly his wounded side was paining him worse than before.

"What do we do, Sammy?" James asked. He looked scared.

Sam made up his mind fast.

"We wait for them right here," he said. "I'll pick 'em off as they ride into the clearing."

"Will you see them, you being half-blind the way you are?"

"Yeah, I'll see them. If they get close enough."

The Kiowa was quiet for a few moments, his face gloomy.

"Sammy," he said, "I got no confidence in you and I got no confidence in your eyes and I got no confidence in your shootin'."

"Hell, Injun, I shot Jeptha Wells, didn't I? If you're so all-fired worried about me, why don't you do the shootin'?"

"I got no confidence in me either," the Kiowa said.

Chapter 22

Lorelei drew rein and leaned toward Hannah Stewart, rain falling between them. She pointed. "Over there. See the arroyo? Maybe we can find shelter."

Thunder roared and drowned out Hannah's reply, but she swung her horse in the direction of the arroyo, head bent against the wind-driven downpour.

The walls of the arroyo provided scant shelter from the rain, but its steep sides cut the wind. Lorelei dismounted and told Hannah to do the same.

"The kid can stay in the saddle," she said. "At least for now."

Hannah, exhausted, wet, and miserable, could only nod, and Lorelei read her strained face.

"How you holding up, schoolma'am?" she said. "All this hasn't been easy for you, has it?"

"I'll be fine," Hannah said. "I'm a lot stronger than I look."

Lorelei glanced around her, at the storm-shredded trees on the rims of the arroyo and then the roiling black sky.

"We'll be all right here for a spell," she said. "Even Dan Wells isn't crazy enough to ride in this weather."

"Is it a box?" Hannah said.

"I don't know. I reckon it is."

"Then if they trap us here, we're done for."

"Unless we get some rest, we're done for anyhow," Lorelei said. "I'm sore wounded, schoolma'am, and I can't ride any further."

Hannah's face paled in alarm as she remembered the bullet in Lorelei's shoulder from Matt Laurie's gun. "Let me see it," Hannah said.

"No, not now, not here. Later." Lorelei led her horse forward. "Follow me," she said. "Maybe there's a place to shelter from the rain up ahead."

The brush and cactus thinned out as the two women made their way deeper into the canyon. After a while it widened and appeared to open up into some sort of clearing.

Lorelei looked back at Hannah and said, "I may have found us a place to camp for the night."

Lorelei walked into the clearing—and immediately came under fire from Sam Sawyer's hammering revolver.

Lorelei's horse screamed and went down in a tangle of legs and leather, shot through the neck. Behind her she heard Hannah's startled yelp of fear. Another bullet split the air above Lorelei's head and forced her to dive for the muddy ground.

"You're killing us here," she yelled.

"Wait, Sammy," the Kiowa yelled. "It's a woman."

"Dang it all," Sam yelled, "I took her fer Dan Wells."

Lorelei rose to her feet. She glared at Sam, her eyes blazing. "Did you fire those shots and kill my hoss?" she said.

Sam stepped toward her. "Sorry. I plumb mistook you for a man."

Lorelei opened her slicker and revealed the breasts swelling under her dress. "You old goat, do I look like a man to you?" she said. She moved to Sam, her face a mask of fury. "Give me that damned gun before you do harm to somebody."

Sam hesitated and Lorelei snapped, "Give it to me!"

Before the woman could say anything else, Sam holstered his Colt and said, "Now, see here, ma'am, I—"

But his words fell on unconscious ears because Lorelei collapsed in a dead faint at his feet.

"Sam, you . . . you killed her," Hannah said.

Taken aback, Sam needed some time to focus on Hannah.

"So, it really was you and little Lori at the Wells place," he said.

"You killed her," Hannah said again. "You shot her."

"Woman not dead, but has bad wound," James said. He knelt beside Lorelei and now looked up at Hannah. "Bullet still in shoulder. Must come out."

"I'm real sorry, Hannah," Sam said, wringing his hands. "I didn't mean to—"

"You didn't shoot her," Hannah said, hugging Lori close. "If she has only one bullet wound, it happened when we were escaping from Dan Wells's place."

"Sammy," the Kiowa said, "bullet must come out."

Rain streamed over them, and the walls of the

arroyo flickered with pulsing light and then darkened again.

"You ever take out a bullet, James?" Sam said.

"No."

"Me neither."

"Well, we can't stand here talking about it," Hannah said. She looked at the Kiowa. "What's your name?"

"You can call me James."

"Right, James. First we have to build some kind of shelter for Lorelei. Can you do that?"

The Kiowa nodded. "Lean-to, maybe, if I can find enough wood. Then we cover it good with slickers."

"Then let's get it done," Hannah said. "Sam, get down to the entrance to the arroyo and keep watch. And for Pete's sake don't shoot any more horses unless you're sure it belongs to Sheriff Moseley or Dan Wells, otherwise you'll set the whole territory afoot."

"Hannah, what happened at the Wells place?" Sam said.

"Later, Sam," Hannah said. "Right now we've got a wounded woman to take care of."

The makeshift shelter was reasonably dry, if cramped. Rain drummed on the stretched-out slickers, and every now and again fat drops fell onto the three people inside.

Hannah cradled Lorelei's head on her lap. The

Kiowa had agreed to do the cutting after Lorelei, who had slowly regained consciousness, turned down Sam's offer, telling him he was so blind he'd cut her throat by mistake.

"Before you start," Lorelei said, "there's a pint of whiskey in the sack on my saddle. Bring it here."

The Kiowa did as he was told and Lorelei passed the bottle to Hannah. "Here, school-ma'am, take a swig."

"Not for me, thank you," Hannah said.

"Take a drink, sister," Lorelei said. "After what you've been through, you need it."

Hannah took a drink from the bottle, coughed, and handed it back.

"It's strong," she said, as though she'd just eaten a hot pepper.

Lorelei nodded. "Matt Laurie made good whiskey, may he burn in hell."

She tilted the bottle to her mouth and drank deep, then drank again.

"All right," she said, "cut away. Just remember that I'm a working gal and I need my shoulders the way they are."

The Kiowa swallowed hard, then dug the point of his knife into the woman's shoulder.

Lorelei screamed.

Chapter 23

"You sure that's the cabin?" Vic Moseley said.

"Yeah, that's the place all right," Dan Wells said. "The breed probably has his Henry trained on us right now."

"In this rain he'll be lucky if he can see a foot outside the damn window," Moseley said.

The sheriff was in a foul mood, hungry, soaked to the skin, and tired of this wild-goose chase to find a man who'd vanished into thin air.

"He can see us, depend on it," Dan Wells said. "The breed can see in the dark like a cat."

"Some say he ain't human," Jake Wells said. "They say he's what the Navajo call a shapeshifter, a man by day an' a wolf by night."

Dan grinned. "I'll tell you what he is. He's half Apache, half Mexican, and all buzzard." He looked at Moseley through the sheeting rain. "How many fingers an' toes you got, Moseley?"

"Twenty, if I'm countin' right."

"You're countin' right. That's how many men Skate Santos has killed, so step careful when you're around him."

"The breed ain't been born yet I'll step careful around," Moseley said.

Dan Wells recognized the empty talk of a hollow

man and said nothing, but his contemptuous eyes spoke volumes.

"Hello the cabin!" he yelled. "You in there, Skate?"

A voice from inside, harsh and demanding: "What the hell do you want, Wells?" A moment's silence, then: "Where's Jeptha? He sneaking around the back?"

"Jeptha's dead, Skate," Wells said. "Shot by a low-down skunk."

Lightning split the dark sky; then thunder roared. From somewhere behind the cabin, a horse whinnied.

"I didn't kill him," Santos said. "Thought about it a time or two, though."

"I know you didn't kill my brother, Skate," Wells said. "But I want you to find the man who did."

"You know my rates," Santos hollered. "Five dollars a day and another hundred if I do the killing. I don't come cheap, Wells, so if you ain't got the money, ride on out of here and count yourself lucky that you still got your hair."

"I got the money, Skate. Now, can we come in and talk? It's wet out here and I could use a cup of coffee."

A silence from the cabin stretched long. Finally Santos said, "Put up your horses in the barn out back. Then come around and walk in by the front door. If I see a man coming at me from the barn, I'll kill him."

"Trusting soul, that breed, ain't he?" Dan Wells said. "One day I'll put a bullet in his hide and kick his teeth in while he lies a-dying."

"Who is he?" Skate Santos said, glaring at Moseley.

"Sheriff from up Haystack Mountain way," Dan Wells said. "You don't need to know his name."

"I don't like lawmen," Santos said. "They stink up the place."

Wells looked at Moseley, gauging his reaction. The man had said he'd never yet met the breed he'd step around.

He'd met one now.

It showed in the way the sheriff sat at the table in the Santos cabin, all drawn in on himself, his mouth a tight gash under his mustache.

The breed was taller than average and muscular. His black hair, as soft and clean as a woman's, fell in glossy waves over his wide shoulders. In an age when men wore mustaches or beards, Santos was clean-shaven.

He wore a pair of ivory-handled Remingtons in shoulder holsters, and a knife hung from a beaded sheath on his belt.

Four years before, during Oscar Wilde's 1882 trip to the United States, a judge in Denver had compared Skate Santos's features to those of the poet. Santos loved the comparison, and after serving three days for assault, he had gone out of his way to meet Wilde and shake his hand.

The breed had a face of a poet, but he had the soul of a killer, and when Moseley met his eyes he glanced quickly away, unnerved by their obsidian fire.

"Who is this man you wish me to kill?" Santos said to Dan Wells.

"Not kill, Skate, track. I want him alive."

"Why did he kill Jeptha?"

"For no reason, Skate," Jake Wells said. "He shot down one of the finest men who ever lived."

"Jeptha was a snake," Santos said. "He needed killing."

Jake half rose to his feet, his face angry, but the breed's smiling taunt froze him. "Do you really want to draw down on me, Jake?"

The big man thought about it for a split second, then sat again.

"Jake, behave yourself," Dan Wells said. "Remember, we're a guest in Skate's house."

"Ah yes," Santos said, "and how remiss of me."

He yelled something in Spanish and a pretty Mexican girl stepped out of the bedroom, her face sullen.

"Coffee for our guests," he said.

"We have no coffee," the girl said.

Santos dropped his head. "Then I am shamed in my own home."

He turned, crossed the floor, grabbed the girl by her upper arm, and shook her.

"Why is there no coffee?"

"The coffee ran out a week ago," the girl said, her eyes defiant. "You know that."

Santos pushed the girl toward the bedroom door. "You shame me, woman. Get out of my sight."

As the girl flounced out of the room, Dan said, "Jake, go get a bottle from my saddlebags."

"No!" Santos said. "I don't allow liquor in my home. It is the drink of the Devil."

Thunder roared and shook the flimsy cabin. When the noise died away to a rumble, Santos said, "You will find shelter in the barn. We will leave at first light."

"We'll head south, Skate," Dan Wells said. "We already tracked north, and the man is not there."

"We'll head where I say we head," Santos said. "Now leave."

As the three men walked their horses to the barn, Jake vented his suppressed rage. "Dan, when are we gonna gun that breed?" he said.

"Soon. When the job is done and we have your brother's killer."

"I want him," Jake said. "And I want his woman."

"Sure, Jake," Dan said, rain running off his hat brim. He looked at his brother like a fond papa chiding a bragging child. "Just make sure his back is turned when you skin iron."

Dan Wells woke from sleep and his hand moved to his gun, a reflex born of his calling. He lay still, listening into the night.

There! He heard it again, the hollow, haunting howl of the hunting wolf.

Gun in hand, Wells rose to his feet. He stepped over the snoring bodies of Jake and Moseley and walked to the door of the barn.

The rain had lessened but still ticked off the top of the doorway and thunder boomed, though keeping its distance.

Off to his left, Wells heard a rustle in the shadowed underbrush. He moved toward the sound, his Colt up and ready.

The wolf howled again, close, and froze Wells in his tracks. Hair rose on the back of his neck, and his mouth was suddenly dry.

A growl, low, menacing, a sound as ancient as time, rose from the brush in front of Wells. No, it was behind him! No, to his right! To his left! All around him!

Wells was tough and he had sand. A lesser man would cut and run, but the outlaw backed toward the barn door, his restless eyes searching the night.

"Show yourself," he called into the darkness. "Be ye man or wolf."

Then he saw it.

A huge animal, black as sin, with eyes like fire.

The wolf loped from the brush into shadow and Wells, relieved, let it go and lowered his gun. Another thing the outlaw life had taught him was not to push his luck.

He heard brush scrape against . . . what?

Was the thing coming back?

Wells raised his gun and thumbed the hammer to full cock.

But it was Skate Santos who emerged through the curtain of the rain, his Henry angled across his chest.

"Dang it, Skate, I could've drilled you," Wells said, his fear maturing into anger. "You know better than to come at a man like that."

"I heard the wolf," Santos said. "I wanted its pelt."

"It was huge, the biggest lobo I ever seen," Wells said.

"Darkness always makes the wolf seem bigger," Santos said.

Wells tried a smile. "Skate, don't you ever sleep?"

The breed said nothing and walked toward the cabin.

"Skate, they say you're a skinwalker," Wells called out after him.

Santos stopped, and then turned.

"Maybe they're right," he said.

Chapter 24

"How is she?" Sam Sawyer said.

"The bullet was not deep," the Kiowa said.

"Why in tarnation don't you ask me?" Lorelei said, lifting her head from Hannah's lap.

"How are you?" Sam said.

"Did James mangle me?"

"No, he didn't," Hannah Stewart said. "You'll only have a small scar."

"Only, the schoolma'am says," Lorelei said. "*Only* a small scar."

She glared at Sam in the thin darkness. "What are you looking at?" she said, the whiskey still in her.

"You," Sam said. He smiled and all the winter fled his face. "I heard you caterwauling all the way to the mouth of the arroyo."

"I reckon you'd caterwaul too if you was bein' butchered by a wild Apache," Lorelei said.

"I'm a tame Kiowa," James said.

"Same difference," Lorelei said.

"Rain's almost gone," Sam said to the woman, "and it will be light soon. We got to move. Can you ride?"

"You shot my horse."

"I know," Sam said. Then almost sadly: "I shot the skewbald pony stone dead. Mayor

Meriwether up at Lost Mine was gonna pay me forty dollars to bring it back."

"That was Meriwether's hoss you shot?" Lorelei said.

"Nah, his daughter's hoss."

"Don't show your face back in Lost Mine again," Lorelei said. "Jerome T. will shoot you fer sure. He sets store by that fat, pimple-faced kid of his."

She struggled to rise and Hannah helped her to a sitting position, but Lorelei fell back again. Lorelei groaned and touched her forehead. "Whoa, too much whiskey," she said. "Let's give it another whirl, schoolma'am."

After a lot of help from Hannah, Lorelei finally got to her feet and carefully pulled the shoulder of her dress over her wound. The Kiowa had bound it up with a bandage torn from Hannah's petticoat, and the bleeding seemed to have stopped.

The rain had thinned to a mist, and the newly bathed morning was coming in clean. Somewhere, gray among the green hills, a wolf howled, then fell silent.

"Lorelei, can you ride?" Hannah said.

"I sure can't walk," Lorelei said.

"We'll let you set the pace, ma'am," Sam said. "When you say go, we go. When you say stop, we stop."

"Got it all figured out, don't you?" Lorelei said.

"I reckon," Sam said, his expression defensive.

"How's all the starting and stopping going to go with Apaches around and Dan Wells on our back trail?" Lorelei said.

"No use building houses on a bridge we ain't come to yet," Sam said.

"So you're a philosopher as well as a hoss shooter," Lorelei said.

"Sammy speak truth," the Kiowa said. "Long ride no good for you, woman. You must take it easy."

"I'll keep up," Lorelei said. "Just knowing that Dan Wells is tracking me will keep me upright on the horse. You better believe it."

Sam Sawyer and the others left the arroyo as the night brightened into morning. To the west a single blue star still stood sentinel in a copper-colored sky, and the clear air smelled of sage and the high timber.

Hannah and Lori rode together, and Lorelei, complaining and cussing, shifted constantly as she tried to get comfortable on the bony back of the Kiowa's paint.

They'd agreed that Silver City was the only place they'd find protection from the Wells brothers and Sheriff Vic Moseley, and the boomtown was now their destination.

"Sam, do you really think there are any Apaches between here and Silver City?" Hannah said.

"Maybe," Sam said. "Apaches come and go. There's no telling where they'll show up next."

"You sound like you fit Apaches before," Lorelei said.

"I did, a few days ago or a week ago," Sam said. "I don't rightly recollect."

"How come you still got your hair?" Lorelei said. "You ain't exactly Kit Carson, are you?"

"I sceered them off, I reckon," Sam said, stretching the truth as much as he dared.

"But, Sam, they took your horse, saddle, and rifle, didn't they?" Hannah said.

"Yeah," Sam said, "on account of how the red devils snuck up on me. Plumb took me by surprise."

Lorelei laughed, then instantly regretted it as she winced in pain. Finally she said, "See, we got nothing to worry about, schoolma'am. Ol' Dan'l Boone here will run off any Apaches we meet. Ain't that so, Sam?"

"That's right," Sam said in a small voice.

"White men talk big when it comes to Apaches," James said. "But when the talkin' is done and the shootin' starts, they ain't so brave."

"I'm sure Sam can handle any difficulties we might have with the savages," Hannah said.

"Do you really believe that, schoolma'am?" Lorelei said.

"Of course I do."

Lorelei shook her head. "Then God help us all."

After he spoke to James about the lay of the land, Sam's plan was to head for the sheltering cliffs of Hell's Half Acre, then swing southeast across rolling timber country directly for Bear Mountain. Once beyond the peak, they'd see Silver City and their salvation in the middle distance.

It was a plan . . . a plan that all too soon would be overwritten by the harsh realities of a hard land and harder men.

Chapter 25

Skate Santos sat his horse and lifted his nose to the wind. "You were right, Indian-eater," he said. "They are not to the north of us."

Dan Wells's anger flared. "Don't call me that, Skate," he said. "I don't like that name."

The breed smiled. "It is said that you ate a Comanche."

"Yeah, a long time ago, and I ain't been that hungry since."

"Then you are an Indian-eater, are you not?"

Wells was mad enough to kill, but he let it go. Right now he needed Santos, but the breed's time would come.

Jake leaned over in the saddle and whispered to his brother, "Now what is he sniffing?"

Santos looked at Jake with his hellfire eyes.

"There is an Apache who sits a gray pony and watches," he said.

"Where?" Dan Wells said, reaching for his booted rifle.

"He is far, and he doesn't see us," Santos said. "He will be there forever, watching."

"Watching fer what?" Wells said.

The breed shook his head. "I do not know."

Dan's anger had cooled some, but still honed him an edge.

"Then tell us something you do know," he said. "Where is the murderer?"

"South, heading for Silver City." Santos hesitated a heartbeat, then said, "But now there are five."

Wells was startled. "Five riders? Five guns?"

"No," Santos said. "Two men, two women, and a child."

"How the hell do you know that?" Jake said.

"In the arroyo I searched, there are tracks of four people and a child. The tracks go south. The women ride, the men walk. One man wears boots, the other moccasins."

"An Apache," Jake said.

Santos said. "No, Kiowa. Only Kiowa sole their moccasins with hard leather, and those tracks are plain to see in mud."

Vic Moseley had been silent all morning. Now

he kneed his horse closer to Dan Wells and said, "Dan, the army payroll leaves Silver City tomorrow at sunup."

Wells nodded. "Yeah, I know. I've been studying and worrying on it for a spell."

"The army will have its usual driver and four armed guards," Moseley said. "But the wagon will be met by a posse from Lost Mine, on account of how Mayor Meriwether heard a rumor that outlaws might attack the shipment."

"Well, fancy that," Wells said, smiling. "Where does the posse link up with the pay wagon?"

"On Bear Creek at Preacher's Point. The posse will take it in the rest of the way."

"How many from Lost Mine?"

"Meriwether told me he'd figured on eight, but I don't know the exact number. There'll be enough, I reckon."

"Then we need to hit the wagon before it reaches the creek."

"I know, but we can't do that if we're chasing all over after your brother's killer," Moseley said. "It's time to make a decision, Dan."

Santos had been listening and now he said, "I will go alone and bring back the man called Sam." He looked hard at Dan Wells. "For a share of the army gold."

Wells thought about that, then said, "What do you reckon, Jake?"

"I want the varmint alive," Jake said.

"He'll be alive enough to enjoy many hours of torture," Santos said.

"He's a sly one, Santos," Moseley said. "Smart as a bunkhouse rat. And it sounds like he's got my woman and her kid with him."

The breed smiled. "He is not clever, lawman. He leaves a trail a child could follow. No, like all men, he got old too soon and wise too late. Dan, I will bring him to your place on the Gila, with Moseley's woman."

"Skate, if the woman is with the murderer, he must've killed Matt Laurie," Dan Wells said. "Laurie was no bargain, so this Sam feller shapes up to be mighty slick with the iron."

"I will bring him, never fear," the breed said.

Jake glanced at the sky, as though the answer to Santos's proposition about a share of the army gold was written in the clouds. A slow-thinking man, he finally gave up and said to his brother, "What do you reckon, Dan?"

Dan Wells made up his mind quickly. "Go get him, Skate, and for Pete's sake keep him alive." He looked at his brother. "I set store by Jeptha, but I ain't letting a thirty-thousand-dollar army payroll slip away from me."

"And the sheriff's woman?" Santos said.

Wells looked as if he felt a sudden pain. "Hell, I don't give a darn about her."

"Moseley?" Santos said. "How much will you pay to get your woman back?"

"Nothing. She's maybe worth a bunch of flowers if it gets her into the sack, but she ain't worth any amount of American cash money."

"Is the child hers?"

"Yeah."

"Will I bring back the child?"

"Hell no. Some other man's get means nothing to me."

Santos dismissed Moseley with his eyes and then turned to Dan Wells. "How big will my share be for bringing in your brother's killer?"

"Whatever you think is fair, Skate," Wells said, his face empty of guile. "You'll find that I'm a reasonable man when it comes to share and share alike."

"Five thousand dollars," Santos said.

Dan Wells nodded and ignored the barbed look his brother threw at him.

"Seems fair to me, Skate. Five thousand it is." He extended his hand. "Done and done."

The breed ignored the proffered hand and swung his horse around. "I will bring back the murderer called Sam in three days. As for the others with him, whether they live or die will depend on my mood and theirs."

"Yeah, well, we don't care about the rest," Jake said. "Get that killer and bring him to me. I want him to know he's gonna be a-dying for a long, long time."

After Santos rode into the shimmering distance of the late morning, Moseley rounded angrily on Dan Wells.

"You really going to pay that breed five thousand in gold?" he said.

Wells's smile was savage. He looked ready to bite.

"Oh, I'll pay the snake all right," he said. "In hot lead."

Chapter 26

The Kiowa decided that a detour into the raw cliffs and narrow canyons of Hell's Half Acre would only slow them down and do nothing to shield them from their pursuers. Instead, in the shadow of McClure Mountain, they crossed Bear Creek and headed due south into the high timber country. They slid through thick piñon and juniper, then into forested areas of mixed conifers and aspens that broke into grassy hillsides and meadows. The air smelled like newly sawn pine, and wildflowers added random fragrances so fragile and fleeting they left no memory behind.

The land drowsed in the heat, still and unmoving, like a gigantic landscape painted in oil by the brush of God.

Fortunately, the swelling in the Kiowa's ankle had gone down and he was able to hobble along fairly well.

Lorelei was no longer cussing and complaining. She had grown silent, her face as white as polished bone, and she stared straight ahead with the unseeing eyes of a marble statue.

"Sam," Hannah said, tearing her eyes from the woman's face. There was a world of alarm in that single word.

Fighting a losing battle with his aching feet and throbbing side, Sam had been lost in his own trudging misery. He looked at Hannah and his expression asked an irritable question.

"Lorelei is sick," the woman said. "I think she's very sick."

Sam took the reins of Lorelei's pony and halted the animal.

"Woman is not real sick," the Kiowa said, stepping beside him. "But she need rest pretty bad."

Sam felt a spike of anxiety. Just one look at Lorelei and it was pretty obvious that the woman was all used up.

But how close were Dan Wells and Moseley?

As though reading his mind, Hannah said, "We must stop, Sam."

Sam voiced his fears. "Dan Wells could be right behind us."

"I know," Hannah said. "But it doesn't alter the

fact that Lorelei still hasn't recovered enough to ride."

To everyone's surprise, Lorelei stirred in the saddle. In a paper-thin voice she said, "Go on without me, schoolma'am. All I'll do is slow you down."

"We're leaving nobody behind," Sam said. "We started this together and by gosh we'll end it that way." He looked at the Kiowa. "Can you build a travois?"

"When I was a boy I saw my mother do it," James said. His eyes moved to a hillside. "Up there beyond the aspen I can find what I need, I think."

"Then get it done," Sam said. "We don't have much time."

"There's a rope on Miz Hannah's saddle for bindings, but rawhide would be better," the Kiowa said.

"Well, we don't have any o' that," Sam said. "Now git goin'."

After the Kiowa left, Hannah, aware of Sam's poor eyesight, led the way into the meager shade of some blackjack pine.

She and Sam helped Lorelei from her horse and laid her on her back.

"How are you feeling?" Hannah asked.

"Like hell," Lorelei said. "That Kiowa mangled me."

"Just lie still," Hannah said. "He's building a travois." She smiled. "You can ride to Silver City in style."

"Like a grand lady in a carriage," Sam said.

"The hell I will, Pops," Lorelei said. "I'll be what I am—a shot-up witch dragging behind a hoss."

"Let me take a look at your shoulder," Hannah said, unbuttoning the other woman's dress.

Sam drew off a ways and built a cigarette, his eyes fixed on his back trail. Blinking like an owl, he peered into the distance but saw only a haze of green earth and blue sky. As near as he could tell, there were no riders in sight, but he wouldn't bet the farm on that being the case.

"What do you see, Sammy?"

Sam jumped, so startled his tobacco spilled from the paper.

The Kiowa smiled. "I like sneaking up on people."

"Gettin' shot is a sure cure fer that," Sam said, sour as a crab apple. He looked the Indian over. "Where are the poles for the travois?"

"I didn't find any, but I found something better."

"A stagecoach, maybe? Or a stalled train deadheading home from Silver City?"

Sam's irony was lost on James. "A cabin," he said. He pointed to the hill. "Up there, just over the ridge."

"What kind of cabin?"

"The log kind of cabin."

"Is there anyone living in the cabin?" Sam said.

The Kiowa nodded. "Yes, I saw a woman draw water from a well."

Sam considered that. "A woman, you say? Sounds like they might be respectable, God-fearing folks living there." He nodded to himself. "Yep, a good place for Lorelei to rest up and a hideout well away from the trail. Surely they'll offer us food and a bed out of Christian charity."

"That was my thinking after I could not find pine poles for the travois," James said.

"Did you know how to make a travois in the first place?" Sam said.

"No."

"Then why did you tell us you could build one?"

"I thought I might be able to figure it out."

Sam shook his head. "You're a mighty useless Kiowa, do you know that?"

"I found the cabin," James said, his mahogany face solemn.

"Yeah, you did," Sam said. "Remind me to thank you fer that later."

"Nice fat lady drawing water," the Kiowa said. "Looks like she cooks fried chicken and biscuits, maybe so."

"Fat ladies always make buttermilk biscuits, the best kind," Sam said. He put a hand on the Kiowa's thin shoulder. "I got a good feeling about this, Injun. A real crackerjack good feelin', you might say."

He had no way of knowing it then, but later those words would come back to haunt him . . . and cause him a world of hurt.

Chapter 27

"Hello the cabin," Sam Sawyer yelled.

Behind him Lorelei sat her horse, supported by Hannah. The Kiowa carried Lori in his arms, and the little girl looked around her with huge eyes.

Sam got no answer and he called out again.

"Hello the cabin! We're weary travelers who need a place to light an' set for a spell."

The cabin was a ramshackle affair that looked to be held together by baling wire and string. It had a sagging roof, a rickety porch out front with a bench, and a couple of rockers. Set off a ways was a pole corral and a barn, as dilapidated as the cabin, an outhouse that looked wide enough to be a two-holer, a toolshed, and a smokehouse.

The cabin had been built in the lee of a jutting, prow-shaped outcropping of rock, and it was shaded by a couple of tall cottonwoods that grew beside a tumbling stream.

"I don't think there's anybody to home," Sam said.

But no sooner had he uttered the words than the

cabin door creaked open on rusty hinges and a woman stepped onto the porch, a riding crop dangling from a loop on her right wrist.

"What do you want?" the woman said. There was nothing friendly in her harsh, low-pitched voice. She stood as tall as a man but was twice as wide, and Sam mentally figured she'd dress out at around three hundred pounds.

"Beggin' your pardon, ma'am," Sam said, touching his hat brim, "but I've got a wounded woman here. She needs a place to rest for a couple of days."

The woman didn't answer. She turned her head and yelled, "Calvin, Cole, Clem, git out here."

From somewhere inside the cabin, a male voice said, "What is it, Ma?"

"You an' your brothers git out here, boy, like I tole you," the woman said. Then, her voice rising to a shout: "Now!"

Three tall, gangling youths barged through the door and tumbled onto the porch. Each wore a holstered Colt and they shared a common expression—the slack-jawed, dull-eyed look of the inbred.

"Lookee what we have here, boys," the woman said. "Pilgrims, an' one o' them right poorly."

"Are them women fer us, Ma?" one of the young men asked, his face eager.

"Bless your heart, Clem. No, they ain't," his ma said. "At least not yet they ain't."

Sam liked nothing about the woman's talk or her sons', and now he tried to back away from it.

"Well, ma'am," he said, "I can see you got a full bunkhouse already, so we'll be on our way. An' I'm right sorry to have troubled you, an' all."

"They call me Ma Capps," the woman said. "And you're welcome to stay the night."

Before Sam could refuse the offer and turn to leave, the big woman's voice stopped him.

"Boys," she said, "get the women off'n them hosses and bring them inside." Then, obviously from experience, she felt the need to clarify that. "I mean bring the women inside, not the hosses."

Her sons needed no second bidding. They jumped off the porch and made a rush for Hannah and Lorelei.

Unfortunately for the man named Clem, Sam was something of a pugilist. Skull, knuckle, and boot fighting was an art he'd learned the hard way and he'd spat teeth into the sawdust after many a knock-down, drag-out saloon brawl.

Clem, his idiotic grin as wide as the wave in a slop bucket, reached up to grab Hannah, but Sam's hard-knuckled fist to the man's bearded chin dropped him cold and drooling on the ground.

Another of the brothers drove a roundhouse right at Sam's head, but he telegraphed the punch and Sam sidestepped. Then he nailed the man in the mouth with a hard straight left.

As the man fell, the third brother, younger than the other two, backed off, his hand clawing for his gun.

"He's drawing, Sammy!" the Kiowa yelled.

Even as Sam hauled iron, a voice in his head screamed, *You're way too slow!*

But as his Colt leveled, a whiskey bottle swung by Ma Capps crashed into the back of Sam's head.

He staggered a step or two, but then his lights went out and he collapsed to the dirt in a heap.

Chapter 28

The cabin was lit with oil lamps that cast deep shadows when Sam Sawyer woke with a splitting headache.

He heard the murmur of voices, at first far off. Then as his consciousness returned, they grew closer. He also became aware that he was propped up in a sitting position against a wall, his hands bound behind him.

The smell in the cabin was horrendous, an amalgam of ancient sweat, the decaying memory of rancid food, and the stench of people who wallowed in their own filth. A breeze wafted through the unglazed back window, bringing with it the odors of the outhouse and the sharp tang of pig manure.

Sam opened one eye, staying perfectly

unmoving as though he was still out of it. Hannah sat at a table in the middle of the room, two of the brothers crowded around her. There was no sign of Lorelei, the Kiowa, or Lori.

A bandanna was wrapped tightly around Clem's jaw, tied in a knot at the top of his head. He sat with his mother, watching his drooling brothers paw and tug at Hannah.

For her part, Hannah made no protest, her face empty, as though this was an ordeal that had to be silently endured.

Sam's anger rose, but he was in no position to intervene. He gritted his teeth and he too made no sound.

The youngest brother, the one who'd drawn down on Sam, jumped to his feet and tried to drag Hannah away from the table.

Ma rose and cut him hard across the back with her riding crop.

"Not yet," she said, over the sound of her son's hurting yelp. "Don't touch her until after the wedding, when it's all nice and legal-like."

"Ma, how's Clem gonna wed us with his jaw broke?" Calvin said, his voice a reedy whine.

"He can say the words"—she turned and looked at her son—"cain't you, boy?"

Clem made a noise between clenched teeth that sounded like "Nunnn . . . nunnn . . . nunnn . . ."

Ma nodded. "Yeah, well, that's close enough for a marrying."

She moved beside Hannah and put a hand on her head. "Calvin, you an' Cole will wed this'n. When the other'n is on her feet, I'm giving her to Clem."

"Aw, Ma, we got to share?" Cole said, a thin, loose-geared man with a matted beard down to his waistband.

"Yeah, you boys will learn to share fer a change. There's enough between her legs fer both of you. You ain't gonna wear it out."

Ma sat at the table again. "I want this cabin filled with young'uns, you hear me?"

"You already got a young'un here, Ma," Cole said.

"I know." The woman looked at Hannah. "What's her name?"

Hannah spoke for the first time since she was dragged into the cabin.

"Her name is Lori."

"Tell her to come over here, to Ma Capps."

"She's asleep," Hannah said.

"Then wake her."

"No, I won't do that."

Ma jumped to her feet, her masculine face twisted into a mask of rage. She raised the riding crop to strike, but Hannah stared at her, unflinching.

Ma's anger fled as quickly as it had arrived.

"All right, dearie," she said, "I don't want a horsewhipping to spoil tomorrow's wedding

157

day." The big woman leaned across the table, her face close to Hannah's. "Bless your heart, child, you don't need to be afeerd o' me. I plan on teaching my brand-new granddaughter all I know about wolfin', scalp-huntin', and whorin' if she's that way inclined. I'll help little Lori make her mark, you can put the kettle on the fire fer that."

"You'll leave my daughter alone," Hannah said, slapping Cole's hand away before pulling her dress closed. "There's nothing a monster like you can teach her."

Ma Capps's hot anger scorched her face.

"Monster, am I?" she screamed. "And me a decent, God-fearing woman as ever was." She turned on Cole. "Take her outside. I'll whip some respect into her."

"Not my wife, Ma!" Cole protested.

"She ain't your wife yet, Cole," Ma said.

"Cole's right, Ma," Calvin said. "We shouldn't whip her."

Ma Capps smiled. "I cain't refuse my boys anything, can I?"

Sam Sawyer roared and tried to get to his feet, but the rowel of his right spur dug awkwardly into the dirt floor and he toppled forward.

For the moment, Ma Capps forgot about Hannah. She rushed on Sam like a great she-bear. Her whip slashed at the helpless man, frenzied back-and-forth blows that cut and stung and drew blood. Ma punctuated her raging screams with every vicious, raking stroke of her whip. "You . . . broke . . . my . . . boy's . . . jaw . . . you . . . piece . . . of . . . trash. . . ."

Sam tried to shield his face by burrowing his chin into his chest, but the whip found his cheeks and forehead, cutting deep, breaking skin. He felt blood trickle onto his neck, and his anger blazed. He threw himself to his left side and kicked out with both feet, aiming for Ma's knees. Both his boot heels made contact and their big-roweled Texas spurs dug deep into her skin.

Ma screamed and staggered backward on suddenly unsteady legs. She crashed onto the table, and then rolled over on Clem. Unable to support his ma's great weight, Clem tumbled onto the floor, and the woman fell on top of him.

Sam heard feet pound toward him and he tried to turn to face this new danger. But it was the Kiowa. Like Sam's, James's hands were tied behind his back.

"Get up, Sammy," he said. "She'll kill you."

James giving him what little assistance he could, Sam struggled to his feet.

Cole and Calvin were trying to lift their mother off Clem, who was kicking and moaning in pain.

Sam looked quickly around him, gathering fleeting impressions of the shadowed cabin.

Lorelei lay on her back on a blanket in the corner to his left, her eyes wide, fixed on Sam. Hannah had Lori in her arms, the child white-faced but too frightened to cry. Outside, the Cappses' cur dog barked and howled in a frenzy and yanked on the chain that bound him to a stake hammered into the dirt.

But Calvin had straightened up, and his gun was in his hand, pointed at Sam's belly.

"They got us buffaloed, James," Sam said. He felt sick to his stomach, from the beating he'd taken or from fear of another. Either way, he couldn't tell.

Ma had hauled her bulk onto the bench beside the table. Like her son's, her eyes were fixed on Sam.

"Want me to shoot him in the belly, Ma?" Calvin said.

The woman's voice was a demonic growl, as though it had been dredged up from the lowest levels of hell. "No," she said, "I want him alive."

Clem sat at the table, groaning as he nursed the broken jaw that his falling mother had reinjured.

"Ma," Cole said, his eyes alight, "here's a fun lark. Why don't we hang him an' the Indian at the wedding tomorrow?"

Ma Capps shook her head. "You can hang the Indian as part of your nuptials, Cole. I don't care." She pointed at Sam. "But I want him skinned. I'll nail up his hide with the wolf pelts."

Cole and Calvin laughed, and even Clem, though it hurt him badly, joined in the mirth.

"Who's gonna skin him, Ma?" Cole said, grinning. "Who, Ma, huh? Huh?"

"Me," Ma said. Her eyes were black ice that froze Sam to the marrow of his bones. "It's been a long time since I skinned a man."

All that was left to Sam Sawyer now was defiance. "All of you can go to hell," he said.

For a few tense moments Sam's words hung in the cabin's stillness . . . only to be blown away by a wind that carried the howl of a hunting wolf.

Chapter 29

"Cole, git your rifle," Ma Capps said. "That there sounds like a big lobo. I want his pelt. The whippin' can wait."

"Ma, are you loco? It's dark out there," Cole said.

"You watch your tongue, boy," Ma said. "Now git the wolf. He sounds big enough an' mean enough to bring ten dollars in Silver City."

"You sceered of the big bad wolf, brother?" Calvin sneered.

"If you ain't sceered, you go get him," Cole said.

Calvin rose to his feet and picked up a Winchester from beside the stone fireplace. "I'll get him, Ma," he said. "A big ol' lobo don't sceer me none."

"Use one bullet, boy," Ma said. "I don't want the pelt all shot to pieces like you did last time."

Calvin nodded. "One bullet, Ma, I promise," Then with a last contemptuous glance at Cole, he opened the cabin door and stepped into darkness.

Ma Capps stood at the window and her eyes searched into the night.

The moon rode high and silvered the wind-trembling aspen. The pines cast arrowheads of shadow that small, gibbering things passed through, rustling from light to dark and back again.

She looked down at Clem. "You hear anything?"

The man shook his head. The bow-tied bandanna made him look like a huge, grotesque rabbit.

"If the lobo's still out there, Calvin will nail him," Ma said. "That boy ain't sceered o' nothin' an' he can track a grasshopper in the dark." She glared at Cole. "Unlike some I could mention."

The wolf howled again, the aching, lonely cry in the shadowed tunnel of the moonlight that wakes a man from uneasy sleep and has him reach for the blue metal comfort of his gun.

"He's behind us," Ma said, her eyes moving. "On top of the ridge."

Cole drew his Colt and stepped to the window at the rear of the cabin and peered outside. He

162

said, "No, I can't," after his ma asked if he could see Calvin.

"Then he's on the lobo's trail fer sure," Ma said. "He'll get him soon. Listen for a single rifle shot like I told him."

The wolf howled, this time longer, louder, and less plaintive.

A few moments passed. Then a terrified shriek rang through the night, like a demon fleeing an exorcised soul.

"Where did that come from?" Ma said, her heavy-cheeked face alarmed.

"I don't know," Cole said. "It sounded like it was all around us."

The man's voice shook a little because, unbidden, an unwelcome guest had slunk into the room—a wan wraith named fear.

"*Yee naaldlooshii*," the Kiowa whispered, his bottom lip trembling.

All eyes turned to him. "What are you saying?" Ma said.

"Skinwalker," the Indian said. "A man in the shape of a wolf."

Cole was shaken. "What do we do?" he said. "How do we kill it?"

The Kiowa shook his head. "Nothing. A shape-shifter is not easy to kill. Now is the time to sing your death song as I will mine."

"Cole," Ma said, "git out there and help your brother."

The man shook his shaggy head. "I ain't goin' out there, Ma."

Ma Capps, her face ugly, went for her son, her whip raised. She stopped in her tracks when something heavy thudded against the cabin door.

"He's coming for you, Ma," Sam said, reading fear in the woman's expression. "The wolf's at the door."

The Kiowa began a low, mournful chant, stone-faced, unmoving. Terror had rammed through him like a lance and pinned him to the spot.

"Better open the door, Ma," Sam said, smiling. "Maybe it's just Calvin wanting back inside in a hurry."

Sam was clutching at a straw. He and the others were in a hopeless situation and he prayed that Ma's and Cole's fear would give him some kind—any kind—of an edge.

Ma held out her hand to Cole. "Gimme the gun, you craven whelp," she said.

The man handed over his Colt without hesitation.

As Ma walked warily to the door, Cole two steps behind her, Sam became aware of someone coming up on his left.

Ma stopped at the door, the Colt hammer back and ready.

"Who's there?" she said. "Is that you, Calvin? Speak up, boy."

Sam felt a woman's soft breath on his neck.

"Stay right where you're at, Pops," Lorelei whispered. "I'm gonna untie you."

Ma lifted the latch and pushed. The door didn't budge.

"Cole," she said, "help me here."

Slowly, like a man wading through mud, Cole stepped beside his ma.

Sam's hands were free. As he worked the stiffness out of his fingers, he felt Lorelei push a derringer into his fist.

"You ain't gonna hit anything with it, but you'll make a noise," she said.

Cole put his strength to the door and it creaked open.

Ma Capps screamed.

Chapter 30

The door swung outward, slowed by its heavy burden.

Calvin Capps hung from a nail by his bandanna, the front of his body pressed against the rough timber. His eyes were wide open, reliving the horror of his last moments.

The man's throat had been torn out. Blood trickled down his chest and legs, and large, scarlet drops ticked from the toes of his boots.

Ma threw herself on her son's body and shrieked her pain.

Cole hesitated at the door. Then, his head on a swivel, he sidestepped outside, doing his best to avoid the body.

It was the last mistake of his life.

A gun roared somewhere in the darkness and Cole went down, a bullet in his chest.

Ma screamed curses at the unseen gunman, and the Colt in her hand bucked as she shot at shadows.

Sam took his chance. He stepped toward the door, the derringer in his hand.

Clem saw the gun and stood, his arms in the air, trying to talk peace, hindered by the tight bandage around his chin.

Sam let the man be for now and reached the door—in time to hear the flat statement of a revolver and see Ma Capps stagger and almost go down. Fat and ungainly, she stumbled outside and fell across Calvin's body. She let out a great sigh and then lay still.

"Stay away from the door, you crazy old coot!" Lorelei yelled.

Sam jumped back into the shelter of the cabin wall.

"You out there," Sam called out. "You hear me?"

"I hear you." A voice from the darkness, hollow in the silence.

"Seems like you killed them all, feller, exceptin'

fer one, an' his jaw is broke, so he's out of the fight," Sam said.

"Is that Ma Capps I just gunned?" the hidden gunman said. "It looked like her."

"Yeah, it was her as ever was. You plugged her an' Cole, an' a wolf done fer Calvin. The one you didn't kill is in here an' he ain't lookin' too good. If'n you're interested, his name is—"

"I know his name."

"His jaw's broke."

"Yeah, you told me that."

Sam measured his words like an inchworm and it was a while before he spoke again. When he did, he said, "Well, feller, we're right obliged to you. Now, if you want to be ridin' on, we'll, in a manner o' speakin', clean up your mess." Sam added a smile to his voice. "We're much obliged to you and when you ride on, be careful. There's a big lobo wolf out there, an' he already kilt a man, so you be careful. An' thanks again an' it's been right nice meetin' you."

"You talk too much," the gunman said. "How many of you in there?"

This time Sam didn't hesitate. "A dozen United States Marshals, all well armed and determined men."

"How many? And this time don't lie to me."

From long experience, Sam recognized defeat when he saw it.

"Me," he said, "two women, one of them

wounded, a young'un, a broke-down Kiowa, an' the feller with his jaw broke."

The voice seemed closer this time.

"Come out here, all of you."

"State your intentions," Sam said.

"I intend to kill all of you if you don't come out here now."

Sam looked at Lorelei. "Think he means it?"

"He's already killed two, maybe three people. I reckon he means it." Lorelei walked to the door. "Don't shoot," she said. "We're coming out."

"I want to see everybody's hands," the gunman said. "If I don't see hands in the air, I'll drill all of you."

"Do as he says, Sammy," the Kiowa said, "and leave the belly gun on the table."

"Maybe I could get the drop on him," Sam said.

"No, you won't," the Indian said. "I have heard the man's voice and I know him. He is Santos, a great warrior and brother to the wolf."

Sam looked into James's eyes, read the warning clear, and said, "I couldn't hit nothing with a belly gun anyhow."

He walked into the night, his hands in the air, like the others.

Clem Capps stood off to one side, obviously frightened. In the moonlight he looked even more like a giant rabbit ready to hop into the brush.

As though he had an instinct for the man's fear, Santos said, "I have no interest in you tonight, Clem. You can return later and bury the ashes of your dead. Go away now."

Clem hesitated a moment, then turned and ran. Santos watched him go, then said, "Put your hands down, all of you."

He hadn't been looking at James, but now he said, "Kiowa, we have met before, I think."

The Indian bowed his head, like a commoner in the presence of royalty. "Yes, Santos, we have. In another place and time."

"We hunted Victorio for the army, did we not?" Santos said.

"Yes, we two and Dahteste, the beautiful one."

"I remember Dahteste well. She was more lovely than any man can describe, yet she was a great scout and a mighty warrior."

"And her spirit was strong," the Kiowa said.

"It was told that Victorio took his own life at Tres Castillos," Santos said. "Is what I heard true?"

James nodded. "That story was told. But the Mexicans say he was killed by hunting wolves, a male and a female."

"Why do you tell me this?"

The Kiowa pointed to the body hanging on the door. "*Yee naaldlooshii.*"

"Your knowledge of the Navajo tongue does you credit, Kiowa. But his throat was torn out by a true wolf," Santos said. He smiled slightly.

169

"I found his body and brought him home."

"Then it must be as you say, Santos," James said, bowing his head again. "You are a great warrior and speaker of the truth."

Hannah, Lori in her arms, stepped toward the breed. "Listen, Mr. Santos or whatever your name is, we have a sick woman here," she said.

"Yes, a wound on her left shoulder that weeps yellow tears," Santos said. His black eyes burned through the moon-gauzed night. "You are the woman of the sheriff, Vic Moseley."

"I'll never be his woman."

"That is well, because he does not want you back. He says dollars are more important than your caresses."

"Then what will you do? Kill me?"

Santos shook his head. "Why should I kill you? You mean nothing to me."

He looked at Sam. "I came for you."

"Dan Wells sent you after me, huh?"

"You killed his brother."

"In a fair fight. He was trying to kill me."

"Dan and Jake want you alive."

"Santos, the only way you're taking me back is over my saddle," Sam said.

"That can be arranged."

The breed spun his Remingtons and both revolvers thudded into their shoulder holsters. "Help me with the wounded woman," he said. "The killing can come later."

Chapter 31

Skate Santos pointed to a grassy spot near a stand of pine.

"We will lay you down there," he told Lorelei. "The cabin stinks and crawls with the souls of dead wolves."

Lorelei was fevered and too weak to protest. Sam helped her onto the ground and gently laid her on her back.

Santos knelt beside the woman and examined the wound. "Who did this to you?" he said. "Who fired the bullet?"

"A low-down snake," Lorelei said.

"His name?" Santos said.

"Matt Laurie."

The breed said, "Does he live?"

"No. I killed him."

Santos nodded. "You did well, woman. You chose the warrior's way, and that is good." He grunted. "The ball was removed by a butcher."

"The Injun did it," Lorelei said.

"Pah, the Kiowa know nothing but horse-stealing and keeping their wives away from other women."

"Why are you helping me?" Lorelei said.

"Because the night is long and I have nothing else to do."

"Big boy, men have told me that before," Lorelei said.

Santos looked at Hannah. "How are your eyes in the night, woman?"

"I can see well in the dark."

"Good. Then I will tell you the plants I need. You will take the child with you. It is good for her to learn such things."

"But . . . but the wolf—" Hannah began.

"He is gone. His hunting is done for this night," Santos said.

After Hannah left, Santos beckoned the Kiowa closer.

"I will need some water from the well," he said. "I will try to undo the damage you have done."

James said nothing. He bowed his head, then turned on his heel and stepped toward the cabin.

Sam knelt beside Lorelei. "How are you feeling, ma'am?" he said.

"Like hell, Pops. How are you?"

"I allow that I've been better."

"We're in a jam, ain't we?" Lorelei said.

"Seems like."

"Yeah. It seems like."

High-level winds scudded frail clouds across the face of the moon, tarnishing their edges like old silver. The air smelled of wildness, of cedar trees and hard-rock mountains, of hidden streams

172

green with fern and moss. And over all hung the smell of burned gunpowder, like the aftermath of an Independence Day street party.

Coyotes yipped in the distance and Santos drew his lips back from his teeth. "Curs," he snarled. "Cowardly, strutting dogs of the night."

Sam cocked his head, listening. After a while he said, "Well, they don't bother me none."

"Then you know nothing," Santos said.

When Hannah returned with an armful of plants and herbs, Santos examined them closely, then told her she'd done well.

He poured a little water in an earthenware bowl the Kiowa had brought him and then added the plants he needed. Some he tore into small pieces; others he pounded with the pommel of his knife until they formed a paste.

"This will heal your wound and help leave the scar smaller," he told Lorelei. "It also dulls pain and cools fever."

The woman raised her head and sniffed the bowl.

"Smells all right," Lorelei said. "Slap it on me, Doc."

"Drink the liquid first," Santos said. He held the bowl to Lorelei's lips.

"You," Santos said to Hannah, "make me a bandage." He handed her his knife. "Cut a strip from your undergarment."

After Lorelei drank the liquid and made a face, Santos spread the herb poultice on her wound.

"You got gentle hands, Doc," she said.

The man nodded. "The warrior should also be a healer. It is the ancient way of the Apache."

He bound the poultice in place with the strip from Hannah's petticoat, then said to her, "I will be gone at first light. You must gather plants and do this until the wound no longer is red with anger." He looked into Hannah's eyes. "Do you understand what I'm telling you?"

The woman nodded.

"Good. Then all is well." To Lorelei he said, "Sleep now and gather strength."

"Whatever you say, Doc," she said, already drowsy. She smiled. "You're the first man who ever laid me on my back and didn't climb on top of me." Lorelei giggled. "It's funny."

"The potion is taking effect and her mind wanders into darkness," he said to Hannah. "She will sleep now and her spirit animal will come to her and help her heal."

He rose to his feet and raised his nose to the wind, his hair blowing across his face. "I must go get my horse. The wolves will come back tonight when the moon rises higher."

Santos gave Sam a hard look. "Don't run. I'll find you, and if I'm angry it might go badly for you."

"Now, that ain't likely, is it?" Sam said, riled. "I ain't going anywhere."

"Afraid of wolves?" Santos said.

"No, just one," Sam said.

The breed laughed. "You are a much wiser man than I thought."

Chapter 32

Skate Santos rode back to the cabin and ordered the Kiowa to saddle a mount for Sam and to release the Cappses' horses from the barn.

The moon climbed higher in the sky, and the shadows shaded deep as Santos dragged the bodies of Ma Capps and her two sons into the cabin.

He found a can of kerosene and poured it over everything that would burn, and then threw an oil lamp against the wooden table. Immediately the table burst into flame and the fire quickly spread.

By the time Santos rejoined the others, the cabin blazed and smoke rose like a column of black marble against the star-scattered sky, a gloomy funeral pyre for Ma Capps and her vile brood.

Santos watched for a while, scarlet flames reflecting in his eyes, then said to no one in particular, "A wolfer's den is a place of evil, but the fire will purify this unholy ground."

Sam said, "Santos, when you get angry at folks, you sure don't get mad and then get over it, do you?"

"Then don't let me get mad at you," the breed said.

"That," Sam said, "is not my intention."

Santos stepped beside Hannah. He held out the derringer. "Is this yours?"

"No. It belongs to Lorelei."

"You take it. You may need it before long. Get close and shoot low."

Hannah slipped the gun into her pocket of her dress. "Thank you," she said.

Santos shrugged. "It is a thing of little account. No need for thanks."

He turned and walked to a saddled mount. "You do not like the horses in the Cappses' barn, Kiowa, so you give Sam Sawyer Hannah's mare?"

"No, I chose this one because Hannah took it from Dan Wells. I'm returning his property."

"Wells took it from someone else."

"As you say, Santos, but by returning it to him he may look kindly on me in the future."

The breed smiled. "You fear me, do you not?"

"Yes. I fear all of your kind."

"There are no skinwalkers among the Kiowa?"

"Yes, there are a few. Some are good, some evil. All are great lords."

"You are a man who gives respect."

"Respect is what I owe, but it is not a thing I give freely."

"Nevertheless, one day I will remember this talk, and it will stand you in good stead."

The Kiowa bowed his head. "You are *Yee naaldlooshii*. You are a man of your word."

"But I am just a man, like you."

"Yes, a man, but not like me."

Santos looked at the burning cabin for a few moments, then again turned to the Kiowa.

"Guide the women and the child to Silver City," he said. "Do not look to save the man named Sam. He is already dead."

"He is a good man, and brave," the Kiowa said. Then, as an afterthought: "Sometimes he is brave."

"I have killed many good and brave men," Santos said. "It has never troubled me."

Lori Stewart held on to her mother's skirt with one hand, the thumb of the other planted firmly in her mouth.

She was sorry to see Sam leave, because she liked him, even though he didn't smell very good. She didn't like the other man who went away with him. He didn't smell good either, like a wet dog.

The lady who was sick was sleeping, and Lori turned her head to look at her. She was a pretty lady, not as pretty as her ma, but she had nice hair and Lori wanted hair like that. But her ma always cut her hair short because it got tangles in it.

Ma said she shouldn't listen to the sick lady too much because she was a cusser and that was a sin, but Lori liked her because sometimes she said funny things.

Lori's eyes moved to the Indian who was watching the cabin burn down. The Indian told her that he had a little girl and her name meant Evening Star. Lori would have liked a name like that, but one day when she was a big girl, Ma said, she could have a pony and she planned to name her Evening Star.

She wondered if the Indian would mind using his daughter's name for a pony. She didn't know, but he was a nice man and she was sure he wouldn't mind at all.

Ma said all the bad people who had lived in the cabin had died and gone to heaven and Lori was happy that they'd gone because they'd scared her, especially the fat lady who looked like a man and had a big, loud voice.

Now Ma was moving and she held tighter to her skirt and went with her.

"Does he have a chance, any chance at all?" Hannah said.

The Kiowa shook his head. "None. If Sammy tries to escape, Santos will hunt him as a wolf and then kill him as a man."

An errant breeze drifted smoke from the burning cabin, and Hannah caught a lungful and coughed.

The Indian, as silent and patient as a bronze statue, waited for the woman to speak again.

"We must do something, James," Hannah said finally.

"We can go to Silver City and tell the law," the Kiowa said. "They will send out a posse, maybe so."

"But Sam Sawyer will be dead by then."

"Santos says he's already dead."

Hannah considered that and her eyes searched the Indian's face, as though she expected to find inspiration there. It was like gazing into an empty rock quarry.

She made up her own mind.

"I'm going after him," she said. "I won't let anything happen to Sam if I can prevent it."

The Kiowa came at that from an angle. "You love him?"

"I don't know." The cabin fire bathed the right side of Hannah's face in crimson light. "I'm not free to love anyone. My husband is still alive." She added, "Wherever he is."

"But you love your child? Of that you are sure?"

"Yes, of course I do."

"Then your place is here with her." James sighed, like a man staring into a future that made him afraid. "I will go in your place."

"Yeah, like one skinny Injun is gonna free the

old coot from Skate Santos, then take on the Wells brothers and Vic Moseley."

Lorelei stood in the firelight and cast a slim shadow.

"Schoolma'am," she said, "for the life of me I don't know why, but if your heart's set on saving Sam's hide, we'll all go."

"You can't go anywhere for a few days," Hannah said. "You're sick and you must rest."

"Hell no. I'd rather die standing up than on my back."

Lorelei moved closer to the other woman. "You were talking about your husband being alive," she said. "I thought you knew."

"Knew what?" Hannah said, on a rising note of alarm.

"Schoolma'am, he's—" She glanced at the child and spelled it out. "D-e-a-d."

"But . . . but . . . when . . . how . . ."

"Vic Moseley said he told you."

"He told me nothing. What happened to Tom?"

"As Sheriff Moseley tells it, he found two bodies in the foothills of the Mule Mountains. He said Apaches had done for them, and that he buried what was left of the remains where they lay."

"He said he found two bodies?"

"Yeah, one was your husband, the other a girl by the name of Sally Burrows."

It took a while for that to sink into Hannah's

consciousness. Then she said, "Why didn't Vic Moseley tell me?"

"Maybe he was trying to spare your feelings."

"Or . . ."

"Yeah, or maybe it wasn't Apaches that done the killings but good ol' Vic hisself. He wanted your husband out of the way and finally saw his chance and took it."

"So he could marry me?"

Lorelei's laugh was scornful.

"I don't understand you," Hannah said.

"Of course you don't understand me. Moseley didn't want to marry you. So long as you thought your husband was alive, Vic could do what he wanted without the complication of a wedding ring."

For a while Hannah looked stunned, unbelieving.

But what Hannah uttered next surprised even the hard-bitten Lorelei.

"I'm going to kill Moseley," she said. "Even if it takes me the rest of my life."

Chapter 33

The afternoon was hot and dust lay heavy on the trail as Sam Sawyer and Santos rode toward the peaks of the Pinos Altos Range. Beyond, the Mogollons rose purple against the sky, like the backbone of a gigantic hunchback.

The breed was not a talking man, and the morning had passed in silence. Sam, much given to pleasant conversation, decided it was high time to be sociable.

He took the makings from his shirt pocket and said, "You smoke, Santos?"

The man's only answer was a shake of the head.

"I was teached how to smoke by vaqueros when I was a younker," Sam said. "They have a great fondness for tobacco and they passed it on to the Texas punchers."

"More fool them," Santos said.

"Oh, I don't know about that," Sam said. "Doctors say smoke is good for the chest, keeps a man's breathing tubes clear."

"What do doctors know?"

Sam lit his cigarette. "They know a lot. Hell, one time a doc down on the Canadian fixed me up after I broke a leg. He told me, 'Son, broken legs go with the cowboyin' profession, and so do broken necks.'"

Sam nodded. "Yep, I never forgot that, because them were words of wisdom. What do you think, Santos?"

"I think you talk too much."

"Well, now, you sure know how to dam up a discussion in midstream, don't you?" Sam said.

But Santos wasn't listening. His eyes were

fixed on the grass and aspen hill country ahead of him.

The breed drew rein and Sam did the same.

"What are you looking at, Santos?" he said.

"Apaches."

"We makin' a run fer it?"

"No. I will talk to them."

Sam was taken aback. "Since you ain't a talkin' feller, and Apaches are pretty much inclined the same way, what the hell are you going to say to each other?"

"Be silent," Santos said. "You are the one in danger, not me." After a few moments, Santos said, "They're Mescalero, my mother's people."

"Well, that's good news," Sam said. "Ain't it?"

"No, the Mescalero stoned her to death for adultery."

Sam groaned. "Well, if you don't mind, Santos, I reckon I'll light a shuck out of here."

"No, you won't. Try to make a break and I'll kill you."

A tense couple of minutes passed, and then it was too late for Sam to go anywhere.

The Apaches, lithe sun-browned men, spread out in a skirmish line and stopped when they were a few yards away. There were seven of them, and they sat their horses silently, their black eyes seeing everything. Sam read a stony indifference in their expressions, but there was something else . . . something tense . . . fearful. The Apaches held themselves stiffly and white-knuckled their rifles as though they were prepared for the sudden onslaught of a dreaded and savage enemy. To a man, they raised their noses and tested the wind and Sam Sawyer had no idea why.

"Right nice to meet you boys," Sam said, smiling. Then in a whisper to Santos: "The little feller at the end is forking my bronc. You reckon this would this be a bad time to mention it to him?"

Santos ignored that and said something in Apache that brought no immediate reaction from the Indians. But after a few moments the oldest of them bowed his head and replied to Santos in the same tongue. His voice was loud and high-pitched, as was the way of the Apache when he talked to someone who scared him.

The talk then went back and forth, and Sam became aware that none of the Apaches had even looked at him. He considered this a good sign, but whether it was or not, he had no idea.

After some speechifying, the oldest Apache pointed to the southeast, then spoke some more.

For a moment Santos looked surprised. Then he said something in return that made the Indians laugh.

The older Apache kneed his pony forward. He bowed again and pulled a heavy silver ring off the middle finger of his right and passed it to Santos.

The breed made a show of gasping in surprise

when he looked at the ring. Then he said something that made the Apache smile.

Santos gave the ring to Sam. "Admire it," he said. "Smile, nod, turn it over in your hand as though it is the most valuable piece of jewelry you ever saw."

Sam brought the ring closer to his eyes and gasped and smiled as Santos had done.

The ring was cheaply made but it was engraved with two interlinked hearts and the words *Mi amor*. Sam guessed it had belonged to some Mexican soldier whose scalp was now hanging in the old Apache's wickiup.

"*Es bueno*," Sam said, dredging up the little Mexican he remembered. He passed the ring back to Santos, glad to get rid of the thing.

The breed slid the ring onto the middle finger of his left hand. He unbuckled the belt around his waist and slid off his English bowie knife with its beaded sheath. He offered the knife to the old warrior, but the man shrank from it and shook his head, as though he'd just been offered a wriggling rattlesnake.

Santos passed the bowie to Sam. "Give it to him," he said.

"He don't want it," Sam said.

"I said give it to him!"

Sam smiled at the Apache and held out the knife. "This is for you, amigo," he said. "Use it in good health."

It looked to Sam that the gift was well received, because the Apache smiled and showed the knife to his companions.

Apaches don't hold much store for elaborate good-byes, so the visit ended when they swung their ponies away and headed west in the direction of the Arizona border.

"We were lucky," Santos said after watching the Indians leave. "The old one told me he remembered me when I was a boy and lived in his *ranchería*. He told me other things, but they don't concern you."

"That was true-blue of him, remembering you an' all," Sam said. "If you and him are almost kin, why wouldn't he take the knife from you?"

"He feared I might want it back and come to his wickiup late at night when the hunting moon is full."

"That doesn't make any sense," Sam said.

"It does to an Apache," Santos said. "He told me more."

"About Hannah and the others?"

"What do I care what happens to Hannah and the others?"

Chastened, Sam made no answer, and Santos said, "The Apache says that early this morning three white men tried to rob an army payroll wagon down near Preacher's Point."

Santos stared to the west, in the direction of the departing Indians.

"Well?" Sam said.

Without looking at the older man, the breed said, "They killed two of the guards, but the firing drew the attention of a cavalry patrol on the scout for Apaches."

Now he turned his head to Sam. "All three of the robbers got away, but it seems a couple of them were badly shot up. The Apache doesn't know who the outlaws were." He smiled faintly. "But I do."

"Kin o' your'n?" Sam said.

Santos ignored that and said, "It was the Wells brothers and Vic Moseley."

That the Wells brothers were involved didn't surprise Sam, but hearing Moseley's name did.

"Hell," he said, "an' I thought they were out lookin' for me."

"You're not that important," Santos said. "And that brings up an interesting question."

"An' I'll do my best to answer it," Sam said. Just before he spoke, he'd briefly thought about jumping Santos and trying to wrestle him to the ground, but had dismissed the idea.

The breed had the face of a preening fop, but the body of a panther. Any way Sam looked at it, he was no kind of bargain.

"The question is addressed to myself," Santos said. "But you may listen."

"Then ask away," Sam said, thinking again.

Maybe he could make a grab for one of the breed's guns. Nah, that wouldn't work either. Santos was as fast as a striking snake. Besides, even if Sam got his hands on one of the Remingtons, he'd be bound to miss with his first shot. The breed wouldn't miss, not with his first or his last.

"Some facts first," Santos said. "Dan Wells promised to cut me in for five thousand dollars from the payroll robbery if I brought you in alive. But now that that venture has failed, all you're worth to me is five dollars a day, say fifteen or twenty dollars."

"An' I'm right sorry about that," Sam said. "I mean, me coming so cheap an' all."

Santos grunted, then said, "Now the question: Is it worth my trouble to keep you alive for twenty dollars?"

The breed lost himself in thought for a few moments. Finally he said, "Maybe I should just kill you, then be on my way."

Sam opened his mouth to speak, but Santos held up a silencing hand.

"No," the breed said, "I've thought about it and have decided that I can't kill you. I promised I'd bring you in alive and a contract is a contract. I have a reputation to uphold."

Santos's eyes whipped the older man from head to toe and Sam felt as if he'd just lost a layer of skin. "You are a trouble to me, old cowboy. I'm starting to think that I regret ever laying eyes on you."

"I'm right sorry to hear you say that," Sam said. "If it's all the same to you, maybe I should just skedaddle and we'll forget this ever happened." He blinked. "I'll send you fifty dollars for your wasted time, just as soon as I get set."

The breed shook his head. "No, it can't be done. I gave my word." He kneed his horse into motion. "Come. We should reach Dan Wells's place before nightfall."

Sam rode knee to knee with Santos and realized where he'd made his big mistake—leaving the Spur Lake Basin country in the first place.

He'd harbored the notion that he might prosper in the restaurant business, and then he'd met Hannah and was smitten by another, better notion—that he might settle down with her and little Lori.

Now both prospects were gone and all that remained were the burned-out cinders of his dreams.

One thing he did know: he'd never let Jake Wells torture him to death. Better a bullet than a branding iron.

Chapter 34

"Look at us," Lorelei said. She'd insisted that everyone link hands in a circle, including the giggling Lori. "Ain't we a posse to be reckoned with?"

Like her daughter, Hannah saw the funny side to the situation.

"I bet about now Santos is shaking in his boots," she said.

"Moccasins," Lorelei said.

And both women laughed.

But the Kiowa's face was set in stone.

"Santos is a great lord and not to be laughed at," he said. "He has killed many men, and he'll kill us."

"The schoolma'am wants her man back," Lorelei said. "There's no stopping a woman when her mind's set on a thing."

"Sam is already a dead man," the Indian said. "Santos told me so."

"James," Hannah said, "we must try to save him. Won't you help us?"

The Kiowa nodded. "I will help. We will die together. It is not for us to know the ways of the Great Spirit, but perhaps that is what he has planned for us."

Lorelei shook her head. "Ain't you just a joy to be around?" she said.

The cabin had burned down to a pile of charred logs, and only a few thin tendrils of smoke rose from the ashes.

As Hannah climbed into the saddle behind Lori, she glanced at the ruin but saw no sign of bodies, and she was relieved about that. Such a sight would have been horror piled on horror.

She felt the weight of the derringer in the pocket of her dress and for the first time realized just how little Santos had given her.

There had been other guns in the cabin, but he had burned them with the bodies, as though he did not want her to be better armed.

Obviously he didn't fear her, so giving her the belly gun had amused him, nothing more, some weird kind of half-Apache humor.

Well, that was your mistake, Santos, Hannah thought. But she realized at once it was false bravado, an empty boast, like a rooster crowing atop a dung heap.

Lorelei had mounted and now she kneed her horse closer to Hannah.

"You're deep in thought, schoolma'am," she said.

Hannah smiled. "I was trying to figure why Santos gave me the derringer."

"Because he's a no-good buzzard," Lorelei said. "He knows if you ever try to use it on an armed man, you'll get killed fer sure."

"Apache humor," Hannah said, giving voice to her earlier thought.

"Yeah, something like that," Lorelei said.

The Kiowa had been unable to round up more of the horses he'd released from the Cappses' barn, so he jogged ahead of Hannah and Lorelei and constantly scouted the trail.

To the north lay the Pinos Altos, and the tracks of Sam and Santos headed in that direction.

Around them the high country stretched motionless and empty, the aspens and pines on the surrounding hillsides standing as still as paper cutouts in the thin morning air.

The Kiowa stopped and when the women rode up on them, he pointed to an area of trampled grass.

"Santos stopped to palaver here," he said.

"Was it with Moseley and the Wells brothers?" Hannah asked.

James shook his head. "Six, seven riders, on unshod ponies. Probably an Apache war band."

His eyes scanned the distances to the west.

"Apaches ride in that direction," he said. "They'll raid into Arizona, maybe so."

The Kiowa's eyes lifted to Hannah and he pointed. "Santos and Sammy head that way, toward Dan Wells's place on the Gila."

A heavy depression settled on Hannah like a sodden cloak.

"Of course that's where we'll find them," she said, in a flat voice. "At the Wells place."

"You having second thoughts about this, schoolma'am?" Lorelei said, her lips pale, paler even than her face.

Hannah needed reassurance, but she found none in Lorelei's fevered eyes or in the blunt, roughed-out features of the Indian.

"We don't have a hope, do we?" Hannah said.

Lorelei ignored that question and asked one of her own. "So, what's changed since we left the cabin?" she said. "Back then you were all for rescuing Sammy boy and putting a bullet into Vic Moseley."

"Maybe now that we're closer, it doesn't seem quite that easy anymore."

"Honey, it never was easy," Lorelei said.

Hannah said nothing and Lorelei laid it on the line.

"We got a kid with us, an Injun who's scared out of his breechclout, a sneaky gun with two bullets in it, and we're up against four of the West's most dangerous gunmen, to say nothing about Apaches."

Lorelei smiled. "So tell me, what was easy about that to begin with?"

Hannah hugged Lori close and laid her chin on top of the child's head. "None of it," she said.

"We go back," the Kiowa said. "Head for Silver City and tell the law."

"And let Sam die," Hannah said. It was not any kind of an accusation, just a statement of fact.

"That about sums it up, sister," Lorelei said.

Hannah was quiet for a long time, her eyes distant.

Finally she said, "Back to Haystack Mountain way, the ghost of an Apache warrior sits his horse among the trees near my cabin. I see him most nights, just sitting there, staring ahead of him into nothing. He doesn't move."

The Kiowa had been listening intently. His face empty, wedged with shadow, he drew off a few yards from the others, stumbling as he walked.

James broke into a low, soft chant and his feet shuffled on the sun-crisp grass.

"Sam thought the Apache was waiting for the return of someone dear to him, and for a while I thought that was the case," Hannah said. "Now I'm not so sure."

Lori watched the Kiowa and smiled around her thumb as the Indian's chant rose and fell amid the hushed morning like a birdsong.

Lorelei waited for Hannah to speak again, her eyes on the Kiowa, saying nothing.

"I believe the Apache failed in some terrible way," Hannah said, "and he was killed before he could make amends. Now he waits forever, hoping to undo the wrong he did."

Her face suddenly quiet, she said, "If I fail Sam, if I turn my back and do nothing, I fear, like the Apache, my soul will haunt this place for all time, forever trying to undo a terrible failure."

Lorelei rounded on the Kiowa. "Quit that racket!" she yelled. When the man's chant fell silent, she redirected her attention to Hannah. "A right pretty speech, schoolma'am, but lay your cards on the table where we can all see them—do we go or not?"

"Yes, but we don't go. I go," Hannah said. "Lori will stay with you and James. You'll find a place to hide in the hills and I'll head to the Gila alone."

"Asking a lot of yourself, ain't you?" Lorelei said.

Hannah smiled. "Maybe, but I'm the only one with a gun."

Lorelei thought for a few moments, then said, "All right, I'm all wore out, so we'll play it your way. But you scout the place well, and if it looks like the deck is stacked against you, then light a shuck the hell out of there."

Hannah smiled. "I will. Believe me, I'm not that brave. It's just that tomorrow and the next day and the day after that I want to look myself in the mirror and be able to say, 'Well, Hannah, at least you tried.' "

"I hope the old coot's worth it, is all," Lorelei said.

She scowled at the Kiowa. "Injun, you'll find us a hideout in the hills where's there's water. Understand?"

"I will find such a place," James said.

"And no more singing, you hear? Blasted chant spooks the tar out of me, makes me think of death and Judgment Day."

"I sing for the dead Apache, that he may find peace," the Indian said.

"Yeah, well, don't do it again. Let him find his own peace without your help."

The Kiowa was as good as his word and led Hannah and Lorelei to a wedge-shaped break in the Pinos Altos foothills where a trickle of water dripped into a stone tank.

Lori, sensing something was amiss, clung to her mother's neck and when Hannah mounted her horse, the child struggled to free herself from the Kiowa's arms.

Lorelei, her face troubled, said, "Schoolma'am, I sure hope you know what you're doing."

Lori broke free of James and ran to Hannah's horse. The woman leaned down and lifted the girl in front of her.

"I'll be back soon, I promise," she said, hugging Lori close. "I'll only be gone a little while."

"I'll go with you, Ma," the child said. "We'll go home now."

Tears reddening her eyes, Hannah said to Lorelei, "Am I doing the right thing?"

"Answering as a fallen woman, my answer is, 'Hell no,'" Lorelei said. "But as a woman who wants to save the man she loves, then the answer is yes."

"I'm not really sure that I love Sam," Hannah said.

"The answer is still yes."

"I'm the only chance he's got. There's only me, no one else."

"Schoolma'am, are you trying to convince me or yourself?"

"Both of us, I guess."

Lorelei reached up and took Lori from her mother. The child immediately kicked and cried, but calmed down just a little when Lorelei told her they'd go pick wildflowers.

"Go," she told Hannah. "Now, before you change your mind."

"Lorelei—" Hannah began.

"It's all right," the other woman said. "I'll take care of her until you get back."

"But your shoulder—"

"Go, schoolma'am! Get out of here and find your man."

Hannah kicked her horse into motion and rode out of the break.

Behind her, she heard her child's cries, and her eyes streamed, as though she were riding into a bitter storm of sleet.

She thought she might go on crying for the rest of her life.

Chapter 35

Skate Santos was not a trusting man.

He pushed Sam ahead of him along the south bank of the Gila, then ordered him to draw rein when the Wells place came in sight around a bend of the river.

Santos took an old-fashioned ship's telescope from his saddlebags and scanned the ledge and the dugouts. There was no sign of life apart from a sleeping hog and a single pecking chicken.

The horses could be in the barn out of sight, but someone should be around at this time of day, Wells's women or a few prospectors down from the Mogollon Mountains.

Santos didn't like the stillness and felt a familiar stirring inside him that warned of danger.

"Nobody's to home," Sam said, sensing the other man's tension. "Hell, Santos, they were all shot up, so maybe they're dead."

Santos made no answer. He loosened the Remingtons in their holsters and slid a Henry rifle from the boot under his knee. He levered a round into the chamber and said to Sam, "We will take a look, me and you."

"Could be a whole passel o' buffalo soldiers lying for you up there, Santos," Sam said.

"Maybe they know you was part of the payroll robbery."

The breed smiled. "Well, that won't matter to you, because once the firing starts I'll kill you."

"Santos," Sam said, "damn me, if you ain't the most unsociable cuss I ever met in my life, and I've met a few."

"Keep talking, old man," the breed said. "You'll be quiet forever soon enough."

Santos made Sam ride ahead of him as they took the ancient talus slope to the rock ledge.

As they walked their horses toward the saloon, they heard the man's screams for the first time.

The grating cries came from the women's cabin. The terrible shrieks were not constant, more a counterpoint to the vile curses the man roared in a high-pitched, pain-shredded voice.

Whoever he was, he cursed himself and the mother who bore him, and he called on Satan to consign all humanity, every man, woman, and child, to the lowest pits of hell.

As Santos and Sam drew rein, the cursing changed, became a shrill wail, the same words repeating over and over again.

"Oh, help me . . . help me . . . help me . . . Oh, somebody help me . . . help me somebody . . . help me . . ."

"What is that?" Sam said. "It's spookin' the tar out of me."

Santos grunted deep in his chest. "I've heard such a thing before," he said. "Only a gut-shot man screams like that."

"Who is it?"

"When a man dies of a belly wound, his voice is no longer his own," Santos said. "It becomes the tongue of pain. I don't know who he is."

"Then God hasten his end, whoever the poor soul might be," Sam said.

Santos shook his head and looked at the older man as though he'd just crawled out from under a rock.

"How did you manage to live this long?" he said.

Sam had no chance to answer. The door swung open and Dan Wells stepped outside. He wore a fat bandage around his left thigh and held a Colt in each hand. When he saw Sam, the hard planes of his face chiseled into a scowl.

"You got him, Skate," Wells said. "You brought him to me."

"Said I would." Santos glanced at the man's thigh. "Caught a bullet, Danny, huh?"

"Yeah, after we stopped the payroll wagon, we was jumped by cavalry. Jake is wounded and Moseley took a round in the belly. I've been listening to him scream and holler like that for hours."

"Too bad," Santos said. He thumbed in the

direction of Sam. "What do you want done with him?"

"Bring him inside and we'll see what Jake has in mind."

Sam felt like a condemned man taking the last step to the gallows. He could see no way out his predicament, unless the cavalry came to his rescue. The chance of that was slim to none, and slim was already saddling up to leave town.

His heart heavy and the fear in his belly tangling itself into knots, Sam was pushed into the saloon by Santos.

Jake Wells smiled when he saw him.

The man's thumb tested the edge of an ivory-handled cutthroat razor, and a hundred different kinds of hell gleamed in his eyes.

Sam heard a scream and for one horrible moment he thought it had come from him.

"How much longer have we got to listen to that?" Jake said, momentarily shifting his attention from Sam to his brother.

"Had enough?" Dan said. "I reckon I've been listening to it for too long."

"More than enough," Jake said. "He's been screaming and calling out for hours."

Dan drew his gun and moved to the door.

"If ol' Vic wants to meet his Maker that badly, it's only fair that I help him along," he said.

Dan stepped outside, and Jake turned his attention to Sam once again.

The man's head was wrapped in a bloodstained bandage and his left leg was propped on a chair. The leg was splinted with split barrel staves and had been bound tightly with rags.

Jake made a show of closely studying the razor.

"Well, lookee here at this," he said. "Says right here on the blade that it was made by Samuel Last, 105 New Bond Street, London." Jake nodded. "The English know how to make razors. They make 'em good an' sharp."

He waved the cutthroat at Santos. "Hey, Skate, you ever seen a man skun with one o' these?"

Before Santos could answer, a shot rang out and the echo bounced through the river canyon like a rock tumbling along a marble corridor.

Jake smiled. "RIP, Vic Moseley." He beckoned to Sam. "Come here, Pops. I want to give you just a little taste o' the blade. I mean, so you'll know what's coming next, like."

"You go to hell," Sam said. His face took on a look of genuine puzzlement. "How come everybody around this here neck o' the woods is hell-bent on skinnin' folks?"

Jake ignored that. "Well, if you won't come to me, then I'll come to you."

He rose clumsily, swayed for a moment, then hobbled forward a step.

Sam moved to his right, booted a chair into

Jake, and the man tripped and fell, roaring in pain as his broken leg slammed into the floor.

Santos was stunned by the suddenness of Sam's move and didn't react before the older man made a dash for the door.

Sam threw the door open . . . then backed slowly into the saloon again, the muzzle of Dan Wells's Colt shoved firmly between his eyes.

"Hold him!" Jake yelled. "Don't let the buzzard go."

Dan holstered his gun and he and Santos grabbed and held Sam's arms. Both were big men, and strong, and Sam's struggles did him no good.

Jake hobbled toward Sam, his face ugly, the razor poised for a slashing cut. "I promised ye a taste," he said, "and now I'll serve it up to you."

It came very quickly, the razor so keen that Sam initially felt little pain. The blade sliced across Sam's right cheek; then a vicious back-handed stroke laid open his left. Blood spurted and Sam saw the front of his shirt turn scarlet.

Jake stepped back and admired his handiwork.

"Finish him, Jake," Dan Wells said. "Cut his throat."

But the younger man shook his head. "No, I want him skun a slice at a time." His bloodshot eyes lifted to his brother. "You and Santos strip him and stake him out. His dying will take many days and he'll scream for all of them, even worse than Moseley."

Sam struggled, and tried to kick out at his tormentor.

"You sorry piece of trash," he yelled. "Let me loose and we'll fight it out, just me and you."

He would have said more, but blood filled his mouth, his head slumped onto his chest and merciful oblivion took him.

"Stake him, Skate," Jake said, "like an Apache would."

"You already owe me thirty dollars," Santos said. "Staking a man will cost you another ten."

Jake smiled. "Then do it. It's well worth the money."

Chapter 36

A lame horse and the buildup to a summer thunderstorm that turned the bright afternoon dark were only two of the problems that beset Hannah Stewart as she made her slow way along the bank of the Gila.

The others were that she had no clear knowledge of the fate awaiting Sam and how she could change it, that and the fear for herself and Lori, chiefly for Lori, that made her drag reluctant feet.

She was close to the Wells place, maybe only a mile or so, and now fear was a constant companion that nagged at her unmercifully.

Hannah unsaddled the horse and turned it loose on grass at the bottom of a hollow, then walked back to the riverbank.

The day had grown even darker, and to the north, in the direction of the Mogollon Mountains, thunder banged and lightning glittered.

The rain came a few minutes later, a steady, wind-driven downpour that hissed on the leaves of the cottonwoods and higher up the slopes made the graceful aspens dance.

Hannah's thin dress soaked very quickly, and when a horseman slowly emerged through the rain, riding toward her, she was uncomfortably aware of the wet cotton. Hannah recognized the rider as Skate Santos, and she stepped into the shelter of the trees. She took the derringer from her pocket and waited.

Santos's waist-length hair hung over his shoulders in sopping braids and he rode with his head bent against the wind and rain.

Hannah waited until the man was a few feet away, then stepped into his path.

"Hands up," she said, realizing how silly that sounded.

Santos drew rein and grinned, both hands on the saddle horn.

"You can put the stinger away, woman," he said. "I'm not going to hurt you."

Hannah kept the derringer trained on the breed.

"Where's Sam?" she said. "Tell me and don't lie to me."

"You know where he is."

"What's happened to him?"

"So far, not too much, though he'll have some new scars on his face."

"Did you do that? Did you harm him?"

Santos shook his head. "No, not me. Jake Wells did it with a razor."

"And you didn't stop him?"

"I wasn't being paid to stop him. Your man means nothing to me."

"Is he in the saloon?"

"No, he's staked to the ground outside the saloon." Santos glanced at the sky. "Not really the weather for that, though."

"Why?"

"Why what?"

"Why is Sam staked to the ground?"

"Jake intends to skin him alive, a little bit at a time." He leaned forward in the saddle. "I tied his wrists and ankles with rawhide, and this rain will stretch it. If you want the save your man, I guess now would be the time to do it. While the rain lasts, you understand?"

"You staked him?"

"Sure I did. Jake Wells paid me ten dollars to do it."

"You're a piece of filth," Hannah said.

And she triggered the derringer.

Chapter 37

Sam Sawyer opened his eyes and stared at a gray sky shot with black that looked so close he could reach out and touch it. He wondered if he could do that, touch the sky and grab a handful of thundercloud, sizzling with lightning. He tried to move his right arm and could not. His wrist was pinned to the ground. Sam tried to move his left arm with the same result and his ankles were tied, his legs spread wide.

The rain hammered into his face and pained him. His cheeks hurt as though he'd cut himself shaving . . .

And then he remembered.

Jake Wells had cut him with a razor, cut him bad, and promised more.

Sam struggled against his bonds, but the rawhide cut into his wrists and the stakes that held them in place refused to budge.

Lightning flared across the sky, and thunder banged a moment later, and it was about then that Sam gave up. He was done for. That was the long and short of it.

He opened his dry mouth and caught rainwater that was cool on his tongue and trickled down his parched throat.

He stared at the sky again, blinking in the

downpour, and wondered when Jake Wells would come for him.

Sam told himself that he wouldn't scream, but he knew he would. No man feels himself getting skinned an inch at a time and does not cry out in pain and fear.

To his right he heard the creak of a door. He turned his head and saw Dan Wells step into the rain. So close was Sam to the door that he could hear the rain drum on Wells's hat and the squelch of his boots in the mud.

Then Wells loomed over him.

"How are you doing, Pops?" he said. He grinned. "I trust you're comfortable."

"You go to hell," Sam said. He could feel his hat still on his head and he thought that middling funny.

"Just stepped out to tell you that Jake will be visiting soon," Wells said. "He's got big plans for you, Pops, big plans."

"He's trash, Wells, just like you," Sam said.

"Big talk from a man lying in the mud who's going to get his skin stripped," Wells said.

He kicked Sam viciously in the ribs, choosing the scabbed-over spot where Jeptha's bullet had burned him.

Wells's boot thudded into Sam again and again and he gasped in pain.

"That was for my brother," Wells said. "But

it's only a taste. Later I'll help Jake with the skinning, and I won't be gentle."

Sam tried to cuss Wells but couldn't, all the breath kicked out of him. He tried to spit at Wells, but his mouth was too dry.

But the big outlaw saw Sam make the attempt and it amused him.

Tall and terrible in the rain, Wells drew his gun.

"Pop! Once right in the belly," he said. "Pretty soon you'd scream like Moseley did. Wouldn't you, old-timer?"

"Go . . . to . . . hell . . . ," Sam managed in a dry croak.

"Nah, a bullet would be too easy, too quick," Wells said. "Best we wait for Jake and his razor, huh? You'd like that, wouldn't you?"

Sam said nothing, but he was scared, more scared than he'd ever been in his life.

Wells's face took on a pretended concern. "Jeez, Pops, I wish I could give you some hope, just a glimmer to keep your spirits up, like. But I can't. All the people you rode with are dead. There ain't nobody coming to rescue you, and that's real sad. I mean, sad for you."

Wells tipped back his head and laughed, great, roaring peals that competed with the thunder and chilled Sam to the bone.

Dan Wells was still laughing when he opened the saloon door and stepped inside.

Despair gripped Sam Sawyer as the downpour lashed at him and the heavy, sullen sky threatened to fall and crush him to a pulp.

Had Wells been telling the truth? Were they all dead? Were Hannah and Lori lying out there somewhere in the wild land, their pale, dead faces turned to the rain?

A great shuddering sigh wrenched Sam's body.

He knew then that he'd lived too long.

It was time for him to die.

The thunder roared and he closed his eyes.

Chapter 38

The .41 round from Hannah's derringer burned across the thick meat of Santos's left shoulder.

The man didn't even flinch and Hannah fired her second barrel.

This time the bullet went . . . well, she didn't know where it went. Nowhere near Santos—that was for certain.

The breed looked at his torn shirt, stained by a streak of blood, and smiled. "You're a regular she-wolf," he said. "It's a quality I very much admire in a woman."

"If I'd two more bullets I'd kill you," Hannah said, her eyes blazing.

Santos nodded. "Yep, I guess you would at that."

He swung out of the saddle and walked toward her through the rattle of the raking rain.

"No," Hannah said, her voice unsteady. She backed away and searched for the hot glow in the man's eyes.

Santos stopped and stared at the ground, shaking his head. When he looked at Hannah again, his smile was still in place. "Why does a woman, especially a homely one, think that every man she meets wants to harm her?"

Hannah was outraged. "How dare you! I'm not home—"

She saw the breed's smile mocking her outburst, and, flustered, she chose the path of least resistance. "Will you give me the road?"

Santos swept off his hat and bowed. "Of course, dear lady."

Soaked, her wet hair falling over her face, Hannah pulled what was left of her dignity around her like a ragged cloak.

"Then I'll be on my way," she said. "If you promise not to follow me."

"I won't come after you," Santos said. "But how will you do it? How will you save Sam Sawyer?"

"I don't know. But I'll find a way."

"Do you have money? Two hundred dollars?"

"Of course not."

"For you, I would kill the Wells brothers for two hundred dollars." He smiled. "My woman's rate."

"I'll free Sam by myself," Hannah said. "I don't need your help."

"No, you won't free him. They'll kill you—or worse."

"Then that's a chance I'll have to take."

"What about your daughter?"

Hannah bit her lip but made no answer.

"She is lucky to have such a mother, and your man is lucky to have such a woman," Santos said. "Aiiiee, you are indeed a she-wolf."

"No, I'm not. I'm scared to death," Hannah said. "Now let me pass."

"Where is your horse?" Santos said.

"He's lame. I let him loose."

"Then you have a long walk ahead of you."

"I'll manage," Hannah said.

"One thing you should know," Santos said. "I used rawhide to bind your man's wrists and ankles."

"What are you telling me?" Hannah said.

"Only that rawhide stretches when it is wet."

Hannah thought about that for a few moments, then said, "Thank you."

Santos said nothing. He stepped to his horse and swung into the wet saddle.

"Good luck," he said, waving a careless hand. He kneed his mount forward and Hannah watched him disappear into the rain and the scowling anger of the brawling day.

It took Hannah the better part of an hour to reach the Wells place on the Gila. The rain had swollen the river slightly and the current was much faster, but she hiked up her skirts and waded across, at one point struggling through rushing water up to her armpits.

Drenched, her hair falling over her face in tight ringlets, she reached the talus slope and started to climb.

Rivulets of rainwater ran down the incline and Hannah dislodged a shower of shingle with every step she took. She fell often and by the time she reached the rock ledge, her dress was covered in mud from neck to hem and her hands were scraped raw.

The storm had not kept its promise of continued thunder and lightning, but rain swept through the surrounding pines and a sharking wind bit deep, its breath cold.

Hannah stepped into the lee of a limestone boulder and her eyes swept the ledge.

Lamps burned in the saloon against the gloom of the day, but there was nothing human or animal in sight. Even the hog had sought shelter.

Then Hannah spotted Sam.

He lay outside the saloon, his arms and legs

spread-eagled, the relentless downpour hammering him. He lay as still as death.

Hannah swallowed hard and tried to wipe rain off her face with her sleeve. The cotton came away pink, her cheek bloodied when she'd fallen on the slope and slammed into loose gravel.

What was it Santos had said? That the rawhide binding Sam's ankles and wrists would loosen in the rain.

She hoped he was right, because she had no knife.

Down below, she heard the rain-swollen rush of the river, and higher up the slope behind the dugouts, spear-pointed pine trees poked holes in the lowering clouds.

Hannah forced herself to move, one small step at a time, wary as a doe at a water hole.

As she got closer to Sam, she saw that the man was not stirring. His head was at an odd angle, forced back on his neck, as though he'd strained mightily against his bonds.

Hannah stepped toward him on cat feet, then froze, her heart racing. She thought she'd heard the saloon door rattle.

"It's the wind," she told herself. "Only the wind."

But fear spiked her to the ground.

Forcing herself to move, she stepped toward Sam again.

To the west, the sky opened a crack, allowing a

watery shaft of sunlight to briefly splash over the rock ledge.

"Oh, please . . . oh, please . . . ," Hannah whispered.

Please don't let the door open.

She reached Sam and knelt beside him. His eyes were shut, and, to her horror, Hannah saw that both of his cheeks had been laid open by a blade. The rain had washed his face clean of blood, but the wounds were deep, red, and angry, like extra mouths.

She glanced over her shoulder at the rectangle of light that was the saloon window, and then began to work on the rawhide bonds.

To her surprise, they loosened easily, not because of the rain, but because Santos had tied them that way.

Hannah didn't take time to fathom the man's motives. Slowed by trembling hands, she untied Sam's wrists and ankles from the wooden stakes and began to drag him away, toward the talus slope.

Sam Sawyer was not a tall man, but he was stocky and solid, and heavy for a woman to move.

Her hands under his armpits, Hannah dragged the man across the muddy ground, her eyes fixed constantly on the saloon door.

Stopping often, rain lashing at her, she was

only a few yards from the top of the talus slope when Sam regained consciousness.

He turned his head and looked up at the woman.

"What are you doing here?" he said.

"Dumb question," Hannah said, breathing hard. "I'm trying to save your life."

"I can walk."

Sam attempted to get to his feet, but his knees buckled and he went down again.

"You've lost blood and it's weakened you, Sam," Hannah said. "Lie still and I'll drag you." She peered through the gray mantle of the downpour. "When we get to the slope, it will be easier."

"Dang it, woman, leave me," Sam said. "If Jake Wells comes out to cut me some more, he'll kill you for sure."

"Shut up, Sam," Hannah said. "I can't spare breath for idle talk."

"Hannah, please, let me go," Sam pleaded.

"Shut up, Sam," Hannah yelled.

By the time they had reached the top of the talus slope, the coming night added to the dark of the day. The slope was running rain like a waterfall, and the air smelled of rotting tree roots and wet stone.

Hannah backed to the edge, dragging Sam, the man's protests just so many meaningless words that didn't register on her consciousness.

The rising wind whipped the woman's hair, the wet strands writhing across her face like Medusa's snakes.

"Hold on, Sam," she said. "We're heading down."

She started to pull again but became a motionless statue when a man yelled from the saloon door.

"You, stop right there!"

"Dang it, Hannah, leave me," Sam cried out. "Save yourself!"

A shot racketed through the dreary dusk, and a bullet spurted mud a few inches from Sam's chest.

Hannah saw a man hobbling toward her, gun in hand, the bandage around his thigh bobbing white in the gloom.

She took a step down the slope, then another, dragging Sam with her. Hannah's breath came in short, sharp, painful gasps and the fingers of both her hands cramped badly, hurting from Sam's weight.

A second bullet split the air inches above Hannah's head, and she tried to hurry her descent.

It was a bad mistake.

The high heel of her lace-up boot rolled on a rock and badly turned her ankle. Off balance, she toppled backward, her arms flailing as she was forced to let go of Sam in an effort to regain her footing.

But the slope was steep, made treacherous by the rain, and she and Sam started to tumble . . . head over heels . . . bouncing down the incline like rubber balls . . . a racketing shower of shingle cascading in their wake.

Chapter 39

Hannah Stewart hit the flat with a thump. She glanced up and saw Sam's cartwheeling body coming at her and quickly rolled out of the way.

Sam's back thudded onto the ground and for a few moments he lay still, stunned, a pulse beating in his throat.

Bullets ripped through the cottonwoods, but Dan Wells was firing blind and none came near.

Hannah crawled to Sam. "Are you all right?" she said.

Unable to speak, the man nodded.

"We need to get out of here, Sam," Hannah said. "They'll come after us real quick."

Sam struggled for breath. Then, like a man choking on a chicken bone, he managed, "Jake's leg is broke. He can't ride. But . . . but Dan will come."

Hannah looked around her, her eyes reaching into the rain-flayed night, but she saw nowhere that suggested a safe hiding place.

"I can walk," Sam said. The razor cuts on his face were gouging his skin like drawn wires.

"But I don't think I can," Hannah said. "I just tried to move my right ankle and it hurt like fire."

"Is it broke?" Sam said.

"I don't think so. But it's sprained maybe."

"The same thing happened to the Injun and he couldn't walk worth a dang fer a long spell," Sam said.

"Well," he said, after a moment's thought, "you're right, we can't stay here. I'll help you."

He rose to his feet. His head swimming, he felt aches horn his body from the top of his head to his toes.

"Sam, are you sure you're all right?" Hannah said. She'd made no attempt to rise herself.

"Yeah, I'm just fine," Sam said. He managed a wan smile. "A few razor cuts and a body covered in bruises, is all." He extended a hand. "Here, let me help you up."

He pulled Hannah to her feet, but she couldn't put any weight on her right leg.

"Hurts bad, huh?" Sam said.

"I'd say considerable."

"We've been dealt a lousy hand, Hannah," Sam said, after he'd retrieved his hat from the bottom of the slope. "And no mistake."

The woman tried a smile that barely moved her lips.

"How do we play it?" she said.

The downpour drummed on Sam's hat and wedged coldly between him and Hannah like a divorce lawyer.

"I don't know," he said. Then, after some thought: "Be full dark soon. We'll find a place to hole up out of the rain."

"I can't walk far," Hannah said. She averted her eyes. "And you're in bad shape."

"Where's your hoss?" Sam said.

"He pulled up lame. I left him"—she pointed north—"that way."

"Put your arm around my shoulder," Sam said. "We'll find some kind of shelter nearby."

Hannah hesitated, and Sam said, "Hell, woman, you've been close to a man afore."

"Only my husband."

"Well, he ain't here and I am. Now lean on me and let's get the hell out of this rain."

As shelters go, what Sam found after a short search wasn't much, a narrow, rocky depression gouged into the hillside, roofed by a couple of fallen pines. The hole in the ground kept out the worst of the wind, and Sam tried to convince himself that there were only a few random drops of rain pattering on his hat.

He ached all over, and his slashed face was also starting to hurt. The wounds on his cheeks were bleeding again, as though he were crying scarlet tears.

Hannah saw and it disturbed her. "Sam," she said, "you're hurt real bad."

"I've been hurt real bad before. Got trampled once by a stampeding herd up Kansas way." He smiled, and regretted it as his stretched lips pulled on his cheeks. Then, talking over some pain, he said, "I thought fer sure I was a goner that night, an' me barely sixteen year old an' skinny as a bed slat."

The depression wasn't large enough for Sam and Hannah to sit side by side, so they faced each other, their knees drawn up.

"You need a doctor, Sam," Hannah said.

"Well, there ain't one around here, is there?" Sam said.

As though jealous that the rain was getting all the attention, thunder ripped across the sky and lightning glimmered among the trees.

After a while, Sam said, "Hannah, why did you risk your life to save me?"

"Because I think I love you, Sam," Hannah said, saying it right out.

"I'm no bargain," Sam said. "And I don't reckon I ever was."

"I don't see any price tag on you."

"I'm fifty years old, Hannah. You need a younger man, someone who'll give you babies and be at your side as they grow up."

"My husband was a younger man and he gave me a baby," Hannah said. "But as soon as Lori began to grow up, he quit on us."

"I wouldn't have done that—quit on you, I mean."

"Look at me, Sam," Hannah said.

"All right, I'm looking."

"Do you love me?"

"That's a helluva question to ask a man."

"Well, do you?"

"I don't know. I've no idea what love is."

"You've never loved anyone?"

"My ma, maybe."

"Sam, love is a desire to be with one person, today, tomorrow, and forever. It feels like a fire, here, in the bosom."

"Maybe I'm too old to feel that way."

"A man is never too old to fall in love."

"A man is never too old to catch measles either," Sam said. "And that don't exactly do him a power o' good."

Hannah was silent for a while. Then she said, "I understand."

"Understand what?"

"That you don't care for me."

"I didn't say that."

Hannah made no answer, and after a clash of thunder, Sam said, "You took me by surprise, Hannah, is all. Let me study on this love thing fer a spell."

"And then?"

"And then I'll tell you if I've caught the bug."

Chapter 40

"Who in tarnation was it, Dan?" Jake Wells said.

"I think it was Moseley's woman."

"Why her?"

"Maybe Sawyer is sweet on her. Maybe he owes her money. How should I know why her?"

"You going after them, Dan?"

"Sure, but not right now. They won't get far in this rain and I'll pull out at first light." Dan Wells looked at his brother. "Do you want the woman?"

"You bet I do, now that all the women of your'n skedaddled."

"I hope I run into them one day," Dan said.

Jake nodded. "Me too. I'll put a bullet in each an' laugh while I'm doin' it."

Dan stepped behind the bar and picked up a bottle. "Drink?"

Jake shook his head. "Nah, maybe later."

Dan poured himself a shot of bourbon, downed it, and poured another. He came back to the table.

"Who do you suppose killed Matt Laurie— Lorelei, Mosley's woman, or somebody else?" he said.

"You care?" Jake said. "What difference does it make? He's dead, ain't he?"

"No difference, just making conversation, passing time."

"Probably Sawyer," Jake said after a while. "When I see him again, I'll ask him."

"When you see him again, skin him," Dan said. "And be done with it."

"I will," Jake said. "Hell, if I'd done like you say, he'd be skun by this time."

A moment later, Jake started in his chair.

"What was that?" he said.

"Just a wolf," Dan said. "Howling out there someplace, hunting jackrabbits."

"Close, ain't he?" Jake's face changed. "Here, you don't think it's—"

"No, it ain't. Santos is a bounty hunter and that's all he is. Forget that skinwalker crap."

"He ain't right in the head, Dan."

"I know he ain't right in the head, an' that's why we're gonna kill him just as soon as your leg heals. You want his woman, don't you?"

The wolf howled again, slicing loud through the lightning-torn fabric of the night as the rain hissed like a snake.

"I don't like that sound," Jake said. "Danged wolf is hungry."

"Wolves are always hungry," Dan said.

Dan Wells stepped to the dugout window and stared into the darkness. Rain rattled against the panes, coalesced, then branched down the glass like the arteries of a skinless corpse.

He thought about Moseley's woman.

His brother had been right. Now that all his

women had fled, he could use the woman as a replacement. For a while at least she'd be worth his two-dollar price. Then he'd get rid of her.

There it was again, the wolf howl.

Dan scowled. Was it Santos trying to scare him?

As soon as he gave thought to that, he dismissed it.

Hell, the breed was already in bed, listening to the rain.

Chapter 41

Sunlight filtering through the trees woke Sam Sawyer with a start.

Across from him Hannah still slept. Her head rested on her crossed arms, and the morning sun had already tangled itself in her hair.

Sam climbed out of the hole, his entire bruised body punishing him. He stood, arched backward, and worked out a few kinks, but a whole passel more remained stubbornly unkinked and he groaned as he barefooted it in the direction of the Gila.

Sam stopped at the edge of the aspen line and studied the trail along the riverbank. As far as his shortsighted eyes could tell, there was no one in sight.

The rain had stopped, but the river was still

swollen and moving fast, showing white water. Eddies caused by outcroppings of rock jutting from the banks slowed the flow here and there, and Sam was sure he saw a wading bird taking advantage of the quieter current, but it might well have been a skinny tree branch.

Sam stayed a few minutes longer. The wind shook the aspens, and a few remaining raindrops spattered on his hat. The morning had been washed free of dust, and Sam thought he could even smell drifting rainbow trout in the river.

He settled his bare butt on a patch of grass and gave in to worry.

Where was Dan Wells?

Had he ridden past already and failed to see him and Hannah in the trees? Or was he hiding somewhere, watching and waiting?

Sam gave up. He had no way of knowing where Wells was, so there was no good gathering bundles of sticks to build a bridge he might never have to cross.

He rose and returned to last night's shelter, where Hannah was already awake, trying to pull back her hair made unruly by rain and wind.

Sam had the tobacco and coffee hunger, but had neither, and his mood deteriorated as the morning wore on. For her part, Hannah seemed lost in thought, her pretty face solemn, her worry about Lori weighing heavily on her.

After some discussion, they decided to stay

where they were until nightfall and then struggle through darkness to rejoin the others.

Until then, all they could do was endure thirst, hunger, and the heat of the long day.

Sam and Hannah spent the morning sitting apart, each wrapped in a dark mantle of misery.

The sun rose higher in the sky, and the tree canopies filtered the light and tinted the slanting beams with color as though they shone through stained-glass windows. There was no breeze; the only sound was the song of birds in the aspen.

Sam drowsed and his head drooped, but suddenly he jerked upright, chilled, his back crawling, like a man who hears footsteps behind him in a graveyard. Hannah felt it too, because she looked at him with wide eyes.

"Stay there," Sam said. Then, thinking about it: "If Dan Wells comes around, tell him I'm dead."

"Where are you going?" Hannah said, her voice rising in alarm.

"I'll scout around. You stay right where you're at."

"Is it Wells?"

"I don't know." He tried to smile. "Maybe we're so scared that we're hearing things, huh?"

Hannah shook her head. "No, Sam. I'm sure I heard a horse."

"Yeah, me too. I'll go take a look."

"Be careful."

Sam made his way down the gradual slope toward the riverbank. Flies buzzed around the open wounds on his cheeks and he had to swat at them constantly.

He went slowly, kept to the trees, and avoided open, grassy areas. Once he even wormed his way through thick brush, the feeling of a malevolent presence so close by driving his fear.

Sam bellied behind a small U-shaped rock ridge rising from a soft carpet of grassy earth. He had a clear view of the riverbank, and what he saw made his heart jump in his chest as the granddaddy of all scares spiked at him.

Dan Wells sat his horse, a rifle across his saddle horn. The man's eyes searched the rise, probing the trees, his outlaw's sixth sense ringing his alarm bells.

Sam swallowed hard.

He knew. Dan Wells *knew*.

After the passage of about a minute, Wells swung out of the saddle and stepped to the bottom of the rise. He stood and his eyes scanned the slope, his body tense.

Sam's mouth drew tight in a bitter line.

Yeah, you son of a gun, you know we're here and you're coming for us.

He watched Wells work his way up the incline, one careful step at a time, the Winchester slanted across his chest.

When the man passed close by, Sam flattened

himself against the earth, his nose pressed in the dirt. He heard the fall of the man's boots come near. Then, as he walked higher up the slope, they faded and finally stopped.

Hannah's little yelp of surprise and alarm followed.

Trying to move as little as possible, Sam craned his head around until he saw Wells. The man was talking.

"Where is he?"

It took a few moments before the woman answered, "Sam is dead."

"How dead?"

"He broke his neck when we fell down the slope in the dark and rain."

"I didn't see his body."

"No, you wouldn't. I dragged him into the trees."

"Why?"

"I didn't want to leave the man I love out in the rain."

"Woman, if you're lying to me, I'll flay the hide off you with a dog whip."

"Look around you," Hannah said. "Sam's not here."

Wells was silent for a few moments, then said, "You come with me."

"Where are you taking me?"

"My brother wants you for his woman. I told him I'd bring you back."

"I won't go with you," Hannah said.

Sam heard her break and run, the scrape of her skirt through the underbrush, then the pounding of Wells's boots as he followed.

Shifting position, Sam eased onto his back. His hand moved and brushed against something hard . . . that rolled away from him.

Without lifting his head, he scrabbled around and his fingers closed on a smooth rock about the size of his fist.

The rock gave him a glimmer of hope, like a man seeing a single patch of blue in a black sky.

The one thing in all his life he could do well was throw a rock.

He stared upward through the tree branches . . . remembering . . . years past . . . when he was a younker . . .

"Hey, Sam," big Dallas Frazer, ramrod of the Circle D, said, "how come that dun hoss has only one eye?"

"Son of a gun wouldn't go into the corral, so I chunked an apple at him," young Sam said.

"You th'ow a mean rock, Sam," Frazer said, " 'cept now you're the proud owner of a one-eyed hoss. Come payday you'll find your wages ten dollars shy."

Despite the fear racking him, Sam smiled to himself. Now he was about to chunk an apple at another, bigger, son of a gun and he hoped his aim was still as true.

One thing for sure, he was a lot better with a rock than he was with a six-gun—even if he was as blind as a coil of barbed wire.

Sam heard the rush of feet through brush. Then he heard Hannah's terrified, protesting shrieks as Wells grabbed her.

Slowly, carefully, he raised his head.

Wells had a bunch of Hannah's hair in his fist, and was dragging her down the slope.

Sam let the man get past, then rose to his feet, his battered body punishing him all over again.

The rock in his hand, he cat-footed after Wells and the woman.

He had one shot, and then he was done. No, worse than done—he was dead.

When Sam got within throwing distance, Dan Wells had his back to him, his left hand tangled in Hannah's hair as he dragged her after him.

But the gunman has the instincts of a cougar, and Wells turned suddenly and let go of the woman at the same time.

For a split second, he clashed eyes with Sam. Then he brought up his Winchester in one fast, smooth motion.

Sam let the rock fly, aiming for the white blur that was all he could make of Wells's face.

Wells fired, a hurried, uphill shot that missed and rattled through the trees.

Sam didn't miss.

The rock hit the gunman smack between the

231

eyes and Wells went down hard, the rifle spinning away from him.

Ignoring Wells, who was struggling to get to his feet, blood from his busted nose running down his face, Sam dived for the Winchester.

He'd had his share of luck, but now it ran out on him.

He grabbed the rifle, but his momentum took him over a dirt ledge undercut into the hillside. Sam fell about four feet, bounced once, then tumbled head over heels down the slope.

But when he hit the flat, he still had the rifle in his hands.

Groggy from his fall, Sam sat up and saw Dan Wells, Colt up and ready, coming down for him, the sides of his boots digging into the soft earth.

Sam stood and levered a round into the chamber of the Winchester.

Wells was about twenty feet away, and at that distance all Sam saw was a vague, man-shaped blur striding toward him.

"You're dead, you old buzzard," Wells said, his scarlet-stained face twisted and ugly. "You get it right in the belly."

He brought up the Colt for a killing shot and Sam triggered the Winchester. He'd no idea where the bullet went.

Hannah saved his life yet again.

She launched herself from the slope and crashed on top of Wells, as he was about to pull the trigger. Both of them fell to the ground, and Wells's shot went wild. Cursing, he slapped the woman away from him and struggled to regain his footing.

Sam had closed the distance between him and the gunman and he fired a second time.

This time the range was shorter and his aim was better. Wells staggered as the bullet hit him just above the belt buckle. Sam fired again, and again, working the lever as fast as he could, and Wells dropped to his knees.

The outlaw held up his hands. "No more," he said. "I'm done. I'm hit hard and I'm out of it."

But there was no mercy in Sam Sawyer that day.

"Die, you Injun-eatin' varmint," he said.

He pumped bullets into Wells until the rifle ran dry; then he threw it on top of the man's lifeless body.

"Damn you," Sam said, all his pent-up fear turning to hate. "Damn you to hell."

Chapter 42

Skate Santos drew rein outside the Wellses' saloon and swung out of the saddle.

Higher up the slope, a flock of piñon jays scouted a stand of hardwoods and he watched them for a while until they settled among the branches.

Santos eased the guns in the holsters, then opened the door and stepped into the rank stench of the saloon.

Jake Wells slept at a table, his head on his arms. His splinted leg was out in front of him, resting on a three-legged stool, and a half-empty whiskey bottle stood at his elbow. So did a .44-40 Colt.

Santos's eyes swept the room. There was no one else around and the tick of the railroad clock behind the bar was loud in the silence.

Rats scuttled in a corner where the brothers kept piles of clothing for sale, pants and shirts and a few pairs of lace-up boots stocked for miners.

Santos walked to the bar, silent in moccasins, and found the cigar box. He selected a Havana, lit it, and then again stepped in front of the sleeping Jake.

Surrounded by a haze of blue smoke, the breed studied the man, smiling. Jake looked like filth, overgrown with hair, his hands and face grimed with ancient dirt. And he smelled like an outhouse.

Still smiling, Santos kicked out the stool from under the man's leg.

Jake woke with a shriek of pain as his foot slammed onto the floor. Then his bloodshot eyes widened as he saw the breed standing over him and he reached for his gun.

But Santos's twin Remingtons were suddenly

pointing at him, the muzzles as big and black as train tunnels.

"I wouldn't, Jake," the breed said. "Or at least I'd take it under consideration before I moved my hand another inch toward the iron."

"You scared me," Jake said. He bent over and tried to rub the knifing pain out of his leg. He lifted his head and looked at Santos. "Why did you do that?" he said.

"Because I don't like you, Jake."

"I never done you no harm, Santos."

"Maybe not. But I saw the way you looked at my woman, and that was harm enough."

Jake poured himself whiskey, drank it down, then poured another.

"You hurt my broke leg," he said. "You hurt it real bad."

"I told you, Jake, I don't like you."

"Are you here to kill me, Santos?" Jake said.

"No." Santos holstered his guns. "I think Sam Sawyer will do that."

Jake Wells laughed, revealing rotten teeth. "That old coot ain't gonna kill me," he said. "Dan is out hunting him right now, and when he brings him back, I'm gonna skin him alive." Jake grinned. "He's bringing me his woman too," he said. A sliver of saliva trickled from the corner of his mouth. "So don't go lookin' fer me for a spell. I'm gonna be right busy." He looked at the breed with rodent eyes.

Santos said, "I think Sawyer will kill you before nightfall, Jake. That's what I think."

"An' I told you, the old man can't take me, not on his best day, he can't."

"You underestimate him, Jake. He's a tough old buzzard."

"What does that mean?"

"It means he's a lot more dangerous than you think." Santos reached down, grabbed the Colt from the table, and tossed it into a corner. "I got to be on my way," Santos said. "I don't need a bullet in the back to push me out the door."

Jake twisted around in his chair. "How am I gonna get my gun? My leg's broke and I think you made it a lot worse."

"Crawl over there into the corner, Jake, and hope you make it before Sam Sawyer gets here."

"He won't come. He's got a yeller streak a mile wide."

"If he has, then he hasn't shown it much," Santos said.

"He won't come. He's yeller, I tell ye."

"Then time will tell if he is or isn't, won't it?"

Santos stepped to the door, then stopped and turned. "Oh, by the way, Jake, I plumb forgot to tell you because it skipped my mind—Dan is dead."

Jake's face showed shock, then disbelief, and then anger. "You're a liar, Santos."

"Suit yourself, Jake."

"I don't like liars."

"Suit yourself again, Jake."

Santos saw wheels move behind the other man's eyes.

"What in blazes happened?" Jake said.

"He got shot."

"Dan's fast on the draw. There ain't nobody can best him in a fair fight."

"Oh, the fight was fair all right, and he did get bested."

"Then who did it? Give me a name."

"Sam Sawyer, of course."

That last stopped Jake cold.

When he managed to speak again, a lump in his throat thinned his voice. "How do you know this?"

"I saw it, late this morning."

"Where was you?"

"High up, in the hills."

"Then how the hell did you see it? Maybe you was mistook."

Santos smiled. "I'm a wolf, Jake, remember? I can see a long ways, day or night." His face took on a sad look as he pretended sympathy. "Face it, Jake. Your brother Dan, as fine a gentleman who ever lived, is deader'n hell in a preacher's backyard. Good news for the Comanche, though. They'll start to get fat again now that the Indian-eater ain't around."

Jake's voice thinned further, into a whine.

"Take me with you, Santos. Be true-blue an' saddle me a horse. Don't leave me a-settin' here with a broke leg."

"Your gun is in the corner, Jake. Like I already told you, crawl over there and pray you get to it before Sawyer finds you."

"Santos, please. At least give me back my iron."

Santos shook his head. "Go get it, Jake. There's a good boy."

"You dirty breed buzzard, one day I'll kill you for this."

"So long, Jake."

Santos opened the door and stepped outside, Jake's curses following him like a flock of frantic birds.

Chapter 43

Birds rustled in the aspens, and the Gila murmured to itself as Sam Sawyer stripped Dan Wells of his cartridge belt and holster and buckled it around his waist. He retrieved the man's fallen Colt and, breaking the habit of a lifetime, loaded all six chambers.

He dropped the revolver into the holster and looked at Hannah when she talked to him.

"We can take Wells's horse and get out of here, Sam," she said.

"It ain't over," Sam said.

"But Dan Wells is dead."

"Yeah, but Jake's shadow still lies on the ground," Sam said.

"Sam, his leg is broken. He won't come after us."

"He scared me, Hannah, scared me bad, and then he cut me. I can't step away like it never happened and live with that."

Hannah said nothing for a while. Then her eyes narrowed.

"You're talking about pride, Sam, stupid male pride. Jake Wells scared you—"

"And cut me."

"And now you have to kill him to prove you're still a man."

"Something like that. I'm still scared, scared right now, but don't chide me, Hannah. It hurts, like you're making me swallow a roll of bobwire."

The woman's voice took on a pleading tone. "Sam, you can't beat Jake Wells in a fight. A broken-down man with a cut-up face isn't going to put the fear of death into him."

Sam glanced at Wells's body, then looked at Hannah, his face no longer clouded. "Take Wells's horse and go back to little Lori. Tell Lorelei and the Kiowa that I'll catch up soon."

"When, soon?"

"When my work here is done and Jake Wells is dead."

He saw Hannah shut down, not wanting to hear any more, but Sam persisted. He touched the scabbed-over cuts on both cheeks with his fingertips. "I owe Jake for this, if nothing else. If I coward out now, do you really think I could ever again be at ease in the company of men?"

It took the woman a long time to answer, and when she did she blindsided Sam and cut into him deep.

"I love you, Sam," she said. "And I don't want to lose you. Am I asking too much of you to love me back and leave this terrible place forever?"

Sam shuffled his bare feet. He was a man who'd never known how to talk pretties to a woman.

Finally he said, "Later, Hannah. We'll discuss the . . . love . . . stuff . . . later." Before Hannah could speak again, he said, "Now, get on the hoss and tell the others I'll be back quicker'n scat."

Hannah sighed her frustration. "All right, then, Sam, I'll see this Jake Wells thing through with you."

Sam shook his head. "No, Hannah, you've saved my life twice and that's enough for any man. Get on the hoss and ride away from here." He smiled. "A tinhorn like Jake Wells ain't gonna get the drop on me."

"I'm going with you, and that's final," Hannah said. She saw the man's hesitancy. "And don't you dare argue with me, Sam Sawyer."

Sam thought about holding out, but the determination blazing in Hannah's eyes convinced him otherwise.

"All right," he said, "let's go finish it."

Sam swung his leg over the saddle. He helped Hannah get up behind him.

"I don't have the voice for it," he said, looking over his shoulder. "Can you howl like a wolf?"

Hannah's surprise registered in her voice. "I don't know. I've never tried."

"You've heard a wolf howl, though, huh?"

"Of course, many times."

"Then let me hear you."

Hannah tipped back her head and let out a loud, plaintive wail.

Sam grinned. "Damn it, that was close enough. Now we have a way to get an edge on Jake Wells."

Chapter 44

Jake Wells bit back pain as he crawled across the saloon floor, his broken leg dragging behind him.

He had to reach his gun. If the breed wasn't lying and Dan was really dead, Sawyer would come after him.

Cursing his helplessness, Jake told himself with every shocking pain that lanced through his leg that he should've skinned Sawyer when he had the chance instead of trying to make the man's agony last.

Down here on the floor, he was at eye level with the rats and he hated them for their ability to run around when he could not. After he found his gun, he'd shoot a few, just to see their bodies explode.

No, Jake, he thought, *save your bullets for Sawyer.* A couple in the belly would slow him down all right, and the buzzard would scream for hours just as Moseley did.

He wormed forward, an inch at a time, his mouth gaping, fighting for breath.

He'd thought about Moseley. Now he considered his woman.

Had he lost her?

Jake had so badly wanted to break her until she willingly did whatever he wanted. Now that opportunity was gone.

Wait! Maybe she'd come here with Sawyer.

Despite his pain and exhaustion, the man grinned.

There was still hope. Kill Sawyer and the woman would give up, surrender to him.

Yeehaa!—he'd have her yet. He'd—

What was that?

Suddenly all thoughts vanished from Jake's head.

There it was again. The howl of a hunting wolf.

Santos was back!

Sobbing deep in his chest, Jake redoubled his efforts. He crawled faster and fear filled his mouth with saliva.

Ignore the pain . . . get to the gun . . .

The wolf howled again, a primal threat as old as mankind that still had the power to kindle ancient fears.

Jake stopped. He turned his head and looked toward the door.

"Santos, you buzzard, I'm gonna kill you," he screamed. "I got my gun back and I'll tack your pelt to the saloon wall."

He crawled again, making a strange "nuh-nuh-nuh" sound, as he bellied closer to the corner.

Finally, after what seemed like an hour of struggle, Jake found his Colt and his hand clasped gratefully around the walnut handle.

He fetched his back against the rock wall of the saloon and yelled, "I'm ready for you, Santos! Come and get me!"

The wolf howled and Jake threw back his head and laughed.

"I ain't scared of a wolf, Santos. I've killed and skun hundreds of lobos, just like you. You hear me, Santos, just like you."

Jake's laugh was spiked with hysteria that choked off as the saloon door burst open, splintering away from its top hinge.

He fanned two fast shots into the doorway, expecting a man—or a wolf—to charge through.

But all he saw was a rectangle of emptiness, a sunlit view of aspen and pine in the far distance.

Jake cursed himself. Two rounds gone and only four left in the cylinder. But they would get the job done if Santos was man enough to show himself.

"Come on in, Santos, have a drink," he yelled, around a laugh. "I'm thirsty."

"Drink your blood, Jake, and your thirst will pass!"

That wasn't Santos's voice!

"Sawyer, is that you?" Jake hollered. "Are you out there with Moseley's woman?"

"You scared, Jake? You sound scared. The wolf gettin' to you, huh?"

"I'm gonna kill you, Sawyer, and then take your woman. I'm gonna skin—"

Jake abruptly shut up. The dawning realization that Sawyer wanted to keep him talking to fix his position inside the saloon silenced the words in his throat.

He grinned to himself. There was only one way into the saloon—through the door. All he had to do was keep calm and bide his time.

Sawyer would come to him, by and by. . . .

Chapter 45

There was only one way Sam Sawyer could get inside the saloon—through the door. But Sam Sawyer didn't have the inclination to walk into Jake Wells's gun.

"The wolf howls didn't work, Sam," Hannah said, "and neither did kicking in the door. Jake didn't come out, and now he can't get at you, and you can't get at him."

"Seems like," Sam said, his eyes moved from the door to the window and back again. "He has more sand than I expected and he's got me corralled."

The listless day was heavy with heat and there was no breeze. Beads of perspiration clung to Hannah's temples like tiny bubbles.

"Sam, let's put some git between us and Jake," she said. "He's no danger to us now."

"He's got to come out of there eventually," Sam said. "And he'll find me waiting for him."

"Suppose he doesn't? Come out, I mean."

"Then I'll go in after him."

"You'll get your fool head blown off."

Sam said nothing, but Hannah pushed it.

"If you charge in there you won't even be able to see him."

"I can see well enough. Anyhow, Jake is a big

target." Sam rubbed his dry lips. "Dang, I wish I had the makings."

"You're irritable, Sam," Hannah said. "An irritable man doesn't think straight."

"No kiddin'?"

"Jake Wells is wearing on you."

"The heck he is, woman. It's the tobacco hunger that's wearing on me."

Sam lapsed into silence, remembering something.

Vic Moseley had been a smoking man.

And that thought led to another . . .

And another . . .

Sam smiled to himself.

Good ol' Moseley would help him kill Jake Wells.

"Stay right where you're at, Hannah, here in the trees," Sam said. "But keep an eye on the door and if Jake comes out, holler."

"What are you planning, Sam?" Hannah said, her face worried.

"I'm going to get Vic Moseley to help me."

"Sam, he's dead."

"I know, and that will make him a right obliging feller."

"But, Sam—"

"Stay here and watch what happens." He laid a hand on Hannah's shoulder. "If I don't make it, git out of here, understand?"

"But, Sam—"

Hannah was talking to empty space. Sam was already running toward the women's cabin.

In life, Vic Moseley had used expensive cologne and English hair pomade and he always smelled good. In death, he smelled pretty bad.

Sam wrinkled his nose as he approached the body.

As far as he could see, the man had two wounds. One was just above his gun belt buckle, still sticky with blood and covered in heaving flies. The second, neater, was right between his eyes, the wound surrounded by a black powder burn, the result of Dan Wells's close-up shot.

To Sam's joy, the makings were still in Moseley's shirt pocket, and there was only a little blood on the full five-cent Bull Durham sack and none on the papers. A further search produced a supply of dry matches.

Sam built a cigarette and dragged deeply, his head swimming a little.

As he smoked he contemplated the body of Vic Moseley, like an unshaven, seedy Hamlet gazing upon the skull of poor Yorick.

Moseley had been a fine-looking man, no doubt about that, with the kind of wavy hair and magnificent dragoon mustache that made female hearts flutter.

Pity he'd been such a dirty, low-down son of a gun.

Sam ground out the butt of the quirlie under his heel and built another.

"Well, Vic," he said, smoke drifting from his mouth as he talked, "you an' me have a job to do, old son."

The man was big, and heavy, and he'd be a deadweight, but Sam reckoned he could handle him, at least over the short distance between the cabin and the saloon.

The body lay on its back on a cot, the eyes open, staring glassily at the beamed ceiling. His cigarette between his lips, Sam grabbed the dead man by the shirtfront and pulled him into a sitting position.

He was hit by a wave of decay's sickly sweetness and was grateful for the smoke drifting into his nose.

Then a problem.

He'd closed the cabin door behind him.

Sam dropped the body again, propped the door open, and stepped back to the cot.

He again pulled Moseley to a sitting posture, spat away the butt of his smoke, and then hauled the dead man to his feet.

Sam grunted from the effort and sweat popped out all over him.

Moseley was even heavier than he'd thought.

He dragged the body to the door, the toes of

Moseley's boots gouging parallel tracks across the dirt floor. Then he was outside in the sunlight.

Breathing hard, Sam propped the body against the wall of the cabin. Moseley's head lolled onto his chest, and his knees buckled, and Sam had a hell of a time getting him upright again.

The heat and the stench of the dead man's decomposing corpse made Sam reconsider his course of action. Maybe it hadn't been such a good idea.

But his poke was empty, and this was his last throw of the dice.

Big Vic Moseley, what was left of him, was his only hope of survival.

Sam manhandled the body away from the cabin, half dragging, half carrying it toward the saloon. His breath came in short, agonized gasps, the effort taking its toll.

Feet pounded to his right and he turned his head and saw Hannah running in his direction, her skirts hauled up to midthigh.

The woman stopped beside him and Sam read the shock in her eyes before she spoke.

"What are you doing?" she said.

"What it looks like," Sam said. "Ol' Vic is gonna help me root Jake Wells out of his hidey-hole."

"Sam, he stinks."

"Yeah, well, he was a stinker when he was

alive. Now help me get him to the saloon door. I'm all used up."

"I wanted to kill him," Hannah said. "Now all I feel for him is pity."

"Yeah, me too," Sam said quickly. "Now help me get the sucker to the door."

Sam thumped Moseley's body against the wall just to the left of the saloon doorway, then rested, his heart banging in his chest.

"Sawyer, is that you?" came Jake's voice from inside.

"Yeah, it's me, Sam Sawyer as ever was." He waited a beat, then said, "Still got your razor, Jake?"

"I'm done with that, Sam. I got a broke leg an' Skate Santos done shot me. I'm taking my medicine like a man an' I don't want to fight no more."

"You giving up, Jake?"

"Sure I am. Like I told you, I'm done."

A thud from inside and Jake said, "I've tossed my gun away, Sam. You can come in now and no harm will come to you."

"That's true-blue," Sam said.

"I'm finished, Sammy, shot through and through. My time is short. Bring your woman and come pray with me."

"Spoke like a gentleman, Jake. Let bygones be bygones, I say. I'm coming in to give you some spiritual comfort."

Sam mustered the last of his strength and

shoved Moseley's body into the doorway. The corpse hung there for a moment, and by the time it collapsed to the sill, Jake Wells had pumped three bullets into its chest.

Ciphering was never one of Sam's strong points, but he added things up and figured that Jake had fired five shots.

Now, praying that the man hadn't filled all six chambers or reloaded from a cartridge belt, he followed Moseley inside, gun in hand.

Sam moved quickly from daylight to gloom and for a few seconds he was blinded, standing motionless just inside the doorway. But from a corner to his left, he heard Jake shriek words at him.

"Sawyer, I'm done. I give up."

Sam's vision cleared as he stepped in the man's direction. He stopped when he made out Jake sitting with his back to the wall.

A miner's boot lay on the floor close to Sam's bare feet, the thud he'd heard when Jake claimed to have tossed his gun.

The man looked up at him, eyes scared. "You've done fer me, Sawyer," he said. "I'm your prisoner."

Sam let his Colt dangle by his side, his face showing no expression.

"Jake," he said finally, "you scared me, and when I get scared bad things happen. One o' them bad things is that I don't take prisoners."

Sam brought up his gun and emptied it at Jake—two hits to the man's chest, one to his left thumb, the others a pair of wild misses.

But it was enough.

Jake Wells, his tongue lolling out of his bloody mouth, was as dead as he was ever going to be.

Chapter 46

Sam Sawyer considered it unfortunate that Mayor Jerome T. Meriwether's wife and daughter were visiting his office when he walked in to tell them about the skewbald pony.

A doctor had stitched up the gashes on his cheeks and covered them with gauze and tape. The mayor chose to ignore Sam's wounds, as though they were of no importance to him.

After an exchange of pleasantries, Meriwether describing Sheriff Vic Moseley as a thieving rogue who was better off dead and Sam telling how that latter was accomplished, the mayor got down to business.

He opened a drawer, removed a tin cashbox, and counted forty dollars onto the table.

"Is the pony outside?" Meriwether said.

His fat kid squealed in delight and ran to the window.

"Papa, he's not there," she said, tears springing into her eyes.

The mayor's wife, a thin, stringy woman who looked as if she lived on scripture and prune juice, sniffed and said to Sam, "Well?"

Sam's shoulders slumped and those parts of his that weren't covered in bandages took on a forlorn look.

"It's dead," he said. "The skewbald pony is no more."

Mrs. Meriwether looked as though she'd just smelled a dead fish.

"What do you mean the skewbald pony's dead?" she said. "Explain yourself."

Sam explained.

"I shot it," he said.

He knew the reaction would be bad, but it was much worse than he'd expected.

The daughter threw herself on the floor, screaming, kicking her fat legs in the air. Mrs. Meriwether, rushing to succor her child, tripped over the spittoon and fell heavily on her face, a terrible cry erupting from her mouth.

Sam stepped around the struggling, shrieking females and said loudly to the mayor, "I reckon my forty dollars is out of the question, huh?"

Meriwether's reply came in the form of a bloodcurdling curse. He grabbed a gun from a drawer and for a moment Sam thought he was going to cut loose.

"Get out of my office! Get out of my town!" he roared above the female bedlam. "If you're not gone from Lost Mine in two minutes, I'll hang you."

Sam Sawyer was a cautious man, and he read the writing on the wall plain enough.

He stepped quickly to the door, but turned and said, "Sorry about the hoss an' all. Just some bad luck."

Another tirade of curses followed him outside.

"I've got two minutes to leave town," Sam said.

"No luck with the forty dollars, huh, Pops?" Lorelei said.

"No," Sam said. "The mayor wasn't in the giving mood today."

Lorelei handed Sam the reins of Dan Wells's horse.

"I guess I'll stay here for a spell," she said. She looked around her. "It ain't much of a burg, but maybe I can start my own house and liven things up a little."

"Lorelei, you're welcome to come live with me," Hannah said.

The woman shook her head. "Thank you for asking, schoolteacher, but I'm a working gal and your kind of life ain't mine."

"Can you find room for me, Miss Lorelei?" the Kiowa said. "Me as a bartender, maybe, an' my wife a cook?"

Lorelei said, "When I get my house, you and your wife have a job."

Sam swung into the saddle. "We got to be

going, Hannah," he said. "I got Meriwether so mad he's about to organize a hemp posse."

He reached down and offered Lorelei his hand. "You take care, now, you hear?"

"You too, Pops, and be good to the school-teacher and little Lori."

"I'll surely do that," Sam said.

He shook hands with the Kiowa. "You're a good one, James, no matter what folks think."

"I'll come by and see you and Miz Hannah," the Indian said. "We'll talk about old times on the war trail."

Sam nodded. "You and the missus will always be welcome."

Sam and Hannah, Lori up in front of her, rode toward the cabin near Haystack Mountain.

As they struck Mogollon Creek and followed it north, Sam turned in the saddle and said, "I've been studying on that love business, Hannah."

"And what did you decide?"

"That I want to spend the rest of my life with you and Lori."

For a few moments, Sam watched the fish jump in the creek. Then he said, "Is that love? I mean me wanting to do that?"

Hannah smiled, leaned from the saddle, and kissed Sam on the mouth.

"It's close enough," she said. "Close enough for me."

Center Point Large Print
600 Brooks Road / PO Box 1
Thorndike ME 04986-0001 USA

(207) 568-3717

US & Canada:
1 800 929-9108
www.centerpointlargeprint.com